THE RHEA JENSEN SERIES

CITY OF ANGELS

BOOK 1

SHERALYN PRATT

D1010394

SPRINGVILLE, UTAH

© 2010 Sheralyn Pratt

The views expressed within this work are the sole responsibility of the author and do not necessarily reflect the position of Cedar Fort, Inc., or any other entity.

This is a work of fiction. The characters, names, incidents, places, and dialogue are products of the author's imagination, and are not to be construed as real.

ISBN 13: 978-1-59955-404-4

Published by Bonneville Books, an imprint of Cedar Fort, Inc., 2373 W. 700 S., Springville, UT 84663
Distributed by Cedar Fort, Inc., www.cedarfort.com

LIBRARY OF CONGRESS CATALOGING-IN-PUBLICATION DATA

Pratt, Sheralyn.
  city of angels / Sheralyn Pratt.
    p. cm.
  Originally published: Salt Lake City, Utah : Spectrum Books, c2003.
  ISBN 978-1-59955-404-4 (alk. paper)
  1. Women private investigators--Fiction. 2. Embezzlement--Fiction. 3. Mormon missionaries--Fiction. I. Title.

  PS3616.R3846S67 2010
  813'.6--dc22

6095 8385 7/16

2010005457

Cover design by Angela D. Olsen
Cover design © 2010 by Lyle Mortimer
Edited and typeset by Megan E. Welton

Printed in the United States of America

10 9 8 7 6 5 4 3 2 1

THE RHEA JENSEN SERIES

BOOK 1

To the fans of *Spies, Lies and a Pair of Ties* . . . I promise
not to be offended if you like *City of Angels* more.

ACKNOWLEDGMENTS

THE TALENTS of so many are to be credited for me having a book with my name on it in your hands. It started with Amber Brewer, who asked me to write this book after reading random scenes over my shoulder one day. Then Camron Wright and Amanda Dickson, who gave me the courage to self publish the first version. From there, Kent Minson and Richard Peterson infused it with professionalism, while Richard Erickson educated me in the publishing business and made a great cover and logo for me! Without Richard, I would have been dead in the water and never even made it to press. Gary Jackson stepped in as another hero, as he's done so many times in my life. Thank you!!! And a special thanks to everyone who bought more than one copy and spread the word . . . there's a special place in heaven for people like you!

This time around, I owe the Cedar Fort team: Angela for the covers, Megan for the great editing, and Jennifer and Lee for liking the books and signing me. Here we go!

ONE

A JOYFUL SOB mingled with the happy chatter of birds in the outdoor restaurant. "Yes!" the woman three tables down on my right cried out, just before leaning to drop a kiss on the man kneeling before her. The proposal and acceptance earned a gentle clap from older couples at surrounding tables.

Ah, romance. Something about it brought people together in ways that bank teller lines, traffic jams, and cramped movie theaters couldn't hold a candle to. There was just something about a proposal that made all the witnesses feel like they were friends for the evening, even if they might flip each other off the next day on the freeway.

In truth, the ambience of the outdoor restaurant was perfect for the romantic retelling of a proposal story. Lighting was provided exclusively by the sun or candle light, and the hanging canopies gave every table the illusion of privacy. Very swank. Add that to the fact that Little Bo Peep's was surrounded by lush botanical gardens, and you had the go-to place for creating a cherished memory. Proposals, anniversaries, celebrations . . . things like that.

And my date was late.

"He's fitting the bill so far," Kyp's voice said in my ear. "I especially like the discrete exit ten feet to your left."

I nodded, knowing he could see my acknowledgment from the camera I'd attached to a rose stem directly behind me that was now broadcasting into his van and recording my every move. Turning my attention back to my phone, I pulled up YouTube and typed "handcuff escape" in the search box.

I'd been on a kick recently to find the easiest way out of handcuffs. All considered, if you had the right tool, it was ridiculously easy. Paper clips, bobby pins, playing cards, and a dozen other everyday objects could do the job. I just wanted to find the least conspicuous one before I made the tool that would attach on my favorite bracelet of all time. It was amazing how functional jewelry could be when you put your mind to it.

"One o'clock," Kyp said in my ear. "Waiter with a wine glass and rose. I think this is our guy."

My heart pounded a few times before I settled it down again. Calm. Timid. I had to look like a pushover or my "date" might back out. I wasn't good at meek, so I hoped my new clothes and Pollyanna hair were helping me out on that front. A Norma Kamali long-sleeved empire dress served as my attire that evening. A Walmart special. It screamed, "Poor as dirt, but trying to hide it" Especially compared to the finery surrounding me. The tablecloth was worth more than my dress, for crying out loud. The ill-fitting cut felt awkward when I moved, but I figured it should get the job done.

"Agatha?" the waiter inquired when he reached my table, using the name I'd given out online.

"That's me," I said, trying to put some farm-girl innocence into my eyes.

"I've been asked to bring this to you," the waiter said as he placed the glass and rose in front of me. "Your date has been detained and should be here shortly. He sends his apologies."

"Thank you," I said as I reached for the drink.

"Is there anything else you would like while you are waiting? An appetizer, perhaps?"

Why not? "Sure. How about a glass of water, no ice, and your feta wraps."

He nodded, his eyes taking note of my dress, probably calculating his tip in advance. "I'll bring those right out, ma'am."

I watched him go and then looked down at the white wine in front of me. From a distance it might look like water, especially in poor lighting, and that's exactly what I was banking on. But first I needed to make sure I had my smoking gun. Reaching into my purse, I pulled out a packet of little strips. The sole purpose of my strips was to test for two of the most popular date-rape drugs, which were also the drugs the man I was hunting had used on his previous victims: ketamine and gamma hydroxybutyrate, aka GHB.

The test is simple, really. You drip a part of your drink onto the tester strip. If it turns blue, you know you're in trouble. If it doesn't, all is well.

"What's the verdict?" Kyp asked even though we both knew the answer. This guy wasn't varying his MO. He thought that using different restaurants and finding girls on different Internet sites kept him safe. Maybe it would have, but he'd messed with the wrong girl along the way. And that girl's dad had hired me.

"Blue," I said, dropping the strip into my purse and picking up my phone. *Little Bo Peep's,* I typed into a new text. *Pick up case summary on right rear tire. It's going down now. Tag. You're it.* After pressing "send," I set the phone down on the table.

Lifting the glass, I swirled the liquid, supposedly to check for residue, as I calculated what to do next. My guy was already at the restaurant. He had to be. It was the only explanation for my drink being drugged, because I wasn't buying for an instant that the waiter had been slipped a twenty to do the deed.

So Mr. Bad was here and most likely watching me. I would have been watching me if I were him. Was he at the bar or peeping through one of the windows from the main building? Had he ordered the drink as if he were going to bring it to me himself and then pretended to chicken out and asked the waiter to do it for him while he pulled himself together? The drink only needed to be unattended for two seconds for him to do what he needed to. No one would suspect a thing.

I really needed the waiter to come back with my order, but in the meantime, I got ready for the switch. I had a little thermos for the wine in the Manhattan-sized handbag I'd picked up with the dress. I removed the thermos and hid it in my lap, ready to capture the wine as evidence. Now I just had to figure out how I was going to do it, seeing as how my "date's" eyes were undoubtedly glued on me by this point, and anything suspicious might scare him off. On the other hand, it was April, and the sun was already disappearing behind the horizon. It was nearly dark. What if he just couldn't see me for a moment? The entire place was candlelit, and I was in a corner with rose bushes, so I didn't have to be worried about being backlit.

The plan was still formulating when the waiter returned.

"Your wraps, ma'am, and a water with no ice."

"Thank you. This will be great."

He looked hesitant to leave. "I'm sure your date will be here soon," he said apologetically. I smiled, regarding him as a witness and wanting him to remember everything as clearly as possible. I shot him a lazy smile.

"He's ten minutes late," I said, checking my watch. "Would you keep me waiting that long?"

He swallowed. "No, ma'am, I don't think I would."

Really? Even with my hair like this? He was blushing. How cute. "Tell me," I continued. "Should I wait? Do you think this guy is worth waiting for?"

His focus shifted to the side, and I could tell he was recalling the man who sent me the drink. When he looked back at me, he gave a small shake of his head. "I think you can do much better, ma'am."

I let my eyes warm as I gave him a once over. "Well, thanks for thinking so."

He nodded and stepped away, not knowing I had just permanently sketched the face of my perp into his brain.

"Should I call the police?" Kyp asked.

"Not until he shows himself," I muttered, trying not to move my lips.

Kyp didn't like my reply. "The guy drugged your drink. That's grounds enough to arrest him. Why shouldn't we call the police? The waiter knows who he is."

I sighed. Some people had no sense of adventure. "Still, wait until I've secured the suspect. It's more tidy that way."

"Rhea, that's the police's job," he cautioned.

"If the police show up, he'll bolt. We've got to close the deal now."

I heard him sigh. "The police aren't going to like you today."

They never did. "Ready?" I said, then conveniently sneezed right onto the candle as my hands dumped the wine into the thermos, twisting the lid on and dropping it back in my purse. I stood, motioning for the waiter to re-light my candle while pouring some of the water from my regular glass into the wine glass to replace what I'd dumped. It took less than five seconds, which hopefully wouldn't spook my guy. Time would tell.

Once my candle was glowing again, I tested my water in the wine glass, just to be sure, and found it drug-free. I downed it, grabbed a feta wrap and my phone, and settled in to wait for my guy while watching some man with a German accent on YouTube explain how to use two paper clips to make handcuff keys for police-grade cuffs. I already knew that one.

"Are you timing me?" I asked Kyp, not looking up.

"Yeah, we're at five."

According to my research, it was reasonable for me to show strong reactions by the ten-minute mark. And with me sitting and given my low body weight, going to sleep was a distinct possibility. Softening my body language, I tried to give the impression I was going lax while watching a kid escape trick cuffs. It went against my instincts not to keep an eye on my environment, but that's what Kyp was for. He was my eyes so I could play my part and not clue this guy into who he was dealing with.

Deciding YouTube had nothing for me, I shut down my browser and placed the phone in my purse while casually pulling out my police-grade cuffs and setting them in my lap under the table.

One minute later, I started blinking drowsily. When Kyp whispered, "Ten," in my ear, I let my head fall to the side. The stage was set. The question was, would my date bite?

"Incoming," Kyp whispered just before I heard footsteps. They stopped at my table and paused a moment before someone blew out the candle lighting my table. My corner was officially dark, and my pounding heart had started the job of pumping adrenaline into my system. The footsteps moved behind me, and the side gate to my left squeaked open, propped open by a rock. No one around us noticed my date's motions, focusing instead on their hushed conversations.

"I knew it," Kyp hissed, and I could tell he wanted to beat this man into the ground. We both read the reports. He knew as well as I the state he had left his previous "dates" in. One false move and I would happily take this guy down myself.

Coming to my side, my suspect caressed my face and spoke.

"You don't look anything like your picture, Agatha." His voice was intimate, soft, almost seductive. He pinched my arm and I nearly flinched. He was testing to see if I was faking and nearly succeeded in outing me. Underneath the tablecloth my

left hand gripped the cuffs. "You're very strong," he said, strok-
ing my arm. "Why do women today try to make themselves
into men?"

In one motion I placed the heel of my right palm across the
back of his hand, pushing his hand toward his wrist as I stood
and cranking his arm behind his back until he was standing on
his tippy toes, instinctively positioning himself so I wouldn't
break his wrist.

"We're strong so we can protect ourselves against men like
you," I said, snapping one of the cuffs on his wrist. He tried
to struggle, but did not cry out when I kicked the back of his
knees to make him fall forward. When his other arm flailed to
fight for balance, I caught it, yanked it back with his other one,
and cuffed it as well. I looked around, making sure no one had
noticed us. They hadn't. We were just a lone couple in a dark
corner while the rest of the establishment ate on.

"You do so much as take a deep breath and I will break
you," I whispered into the man's ear. "Do you understand?"
To my dismay, he didn't even offer a token resistance. He just
nodded like a man who'd been praying to be caught. I liked it
better when they fought.

Leaning away, I spoke again, keeping my voice soft. "Kyp,
have you called the police?"

"I'm talking to them now."

"Tell them I'm taking him out the back gate and we'll wait
for them by the pepper gardens." Maybe I'd make the guy eat a
few while we were waiting. Some were strong enough to make
an elephant cry.

"Should we bring an ambulance?" Kyp asked. "Did you
break anything?"

"Not a scratch," I replied, looking over the man that had
brought so much heartache into the world. Dark hair, receding
hairline, normal face. Just your average, everyday guy trying
not to hyperventilate. Why couldn't sick men like him just

walk around wearing a sign or grow the same facial hair or something?

"Fine," Kyp said. "I'll get the camera and meet you once I get off the phone with them."

"I'll be waiting," I said, wrapping my hand around my date's thumb and pushing the bone straight into the hand joint until he gasped in pain. I had his attention. "We're going to leave quietly now. Do you understand?"

When his head nodded vigorously, I pushed a little harder so he wouldn't get any ideas. "Okay, stand on three. Ready? One, two, three."

He stood, no tricks, and was as docile as a lamb as I led him out the back gate and kicked the rock away from the door to let the gate shut behind us. When I reached out to stop the door from clattering shut and disturbing the diners, he made his move. It was smart of him to wait until I was multitasking, but it was also very predictable. When he chose to rush me rather than just run, I think it was his goal to smash me against the fence and daze me before running for it. Or maybe he hadn't thought that far in advance. I'd never ask, but it was easy enough to twist out of his way and let him run face first into the fence before spinning him around and dropping a strike on the top of his sternum. Air rushed out of him in a sob as he sunk to his knees and fought to remember how to breathe in again. He'd figure it out.

"Upsie daisy," I said, pushing up on a nerve bundle in his armpit. "I said we'd be by the peppers so we've got a little ways to go."

Breaths tripping over each other, the man stood and stumbled forward as I pushed from behind. Kyp and the police would be along any minute and relieve me of this guy, but long before I heard either of them, I heard something infinitely more familiar. It was the voice of a woman I'd known since college, saying:

"This is Kathryn McCoy, coming to you live from a small restaurant in Pasadena, where a serial-rapist has just been apprehended . . . "

Tag, Kay, I thought. *You're so it.*

PULLING UP to my house, I checked for my roommates' cars. Emily was home and Camille was off with her fiancé. Hallelujah! When I decided to take on roommates, I had not anticipated someone like Camille. I could have kicked her out, seeing as how it was my house, but in five months she would be married and someone else's roommate. I could handle her for that long as long as I had Emily there for my sanity.

Emily's daddy pays for everything she wants as long as she stays in college, so she takes about eight credits a semester and spends the rest of her time either out with boys or at home talking about boys. Her mindless blabbering is a good daily reminder that I'm not as old as I feel.

Closing the garage behind me, I entered the house to hear a *Top Model* contender lamenting about a shoot gone wrong and Emily gabbing on the phone.

"So meet at eight? . . . Okay, yeah, that'll be great! . . . Yeah, I've been there before . . ."

She watched me come down the hall and smiled brightly. "Yeah, I'll ask her if she wants to come too . . . Yeah, she just got here. I'll call you back, okay? . . . Okay, bye!" She clicked the phone off. "You're home early from your date."

"Am I?" I replied.

"Yeah." She pointed to the clock. "It's not even nine. And what are you wearing? Aren't those your mowing clothes?"

I glanced down and realized how I appeared. I'd been so happy to get out of my Walmart dress that I'd forgotten that no one went out on a first date wearing shorts and a tank top. Whoops. Normally Emily wasn't so observant. She also wasn't usually home on Wednesday nights either—or any night, for that matter.

"I changed," I said noncommittally. "These were more comfortable."

Emily rolled her eyes and sighed. "I swear, Rhea, one of these days you're going to have to get a job doing more than cutting lawns for your dad at ten bucks an hour."

That's another thing I like about Emily—she's not the brightest crayon in the box. Granted, occasionally I do work for my father doing landscaping and maintenance, but Emily accepts my claim of mowing lawns and being a freelance photographer without the bat of an eye. There are only a few people outside of my family who know what I really do for a living. I don't know why, but I don't like advertising that I'm a private investigator. You never know whom you might end up investigating one day.

"It's fine for now," I said, grabbing a yogurt from the fridge and glancing at the clock while getting a spoon. Of all people, Emily was not one to lecture about employment.

"That was Jenn on the phone. A group of us are going dancing this Saturday. Wanna come?"

I flipped through my schedule mentally. I had nothing scheduled for Saturday, but that doesn't mean much in my line of work. Still, I like dancing and even more so with Emily. I think she was the muse of dancing in a previous life.

"Sounds fun. Count me in as long as my uncle doesn't need me to babysit." That's my traditional cop-out. If work calls, I'm going "babysitting."

"Great, you're coming then! And by the way—" She tossed my cell phone to me over the island between us. "You left your phone home again. Ben called." She wagged her eyebrows, insinuating something that didn't exist, and I laughed as I caught my second phone and scrolled through the missed calls. I don't like getting business and social calls on the same line and am in the habit of leaving my "social" phone home while working a case so I won't be distracted. Emily, who couldn't live a moment without her phone, just thought I was forgetful.

"There's nothing going on with Ben, Em. We're just friends."

I speed dialed Ben, while admitting to myself that our story is a long one for two people with nothing going on. We've known each other since elementary school and dated for a while when we were teens, but ultimately decided that we made better friends. Still, there's no denying Ben is hot, and whenever I'm lacking for a date, I am not at all ashamed to bring him along.

"Ben's phone," came the greeting after the first ring, but the voice wasn't Ben's. Mike was one of the eight other rock star wannabes that cramped into Ben's two-story house, which originally had three bedrooms but now magically has six. It is the ultimate love pad, a place of easy action, so infamous that it had been named "The Niners" after the number of lovebirds who permanently nested there. I think I am the only girl who has walked in and out of that house without getting a little love from someone.

"Mike, right?" I said, listening to Ben picking at his guitar in the background.

"Yeah, I'll get him." He handed off the phone.

"Hello?" Ben said, his guitar louder than him.

"You called?"

The guitar stopped mid-strum. "Hey, Rhea! You're home early!"

He'd known I was on a date? "So they say. What's up?"

"I wrote another song. This one's good, but there's a catch."

I rolled my eyes and took the bait, knowing what was coming. "What's that?"

"I wrote it for a girl to sing."

We both knew exactly what that meant. "Ben, you guys don't need me! You have an amazing voice."

"We've talked about it, Rhea. We all want you!" A loaded statement. Or rather, I wished it was. "Come over and practice with us."

Ben knew I couldn't refuse him, and I was sure he had already told the guys I was coming. For that reason alone I wanted to turn him down, but if I did that, then I would just end up dwelling on him all night. Either way he'd win, so I figured I might as well go jam like old times. But before I did, I had some work I needed to finish up.

"I'll be there in an hour," I heard myself say and inwardly sighed at my lack of will power.

"Great. We'll be here. You'll love this new song."

"I'm sure I will."

"See ya soon!"

I hung up the phone and walked to my room.

"Are you going to Ben's again?" Emily called after me.

"Yeah, in a bit. Why?"

"No reason," she replied smugly.

"No reason," I parroted.

No one believes Ben and I are just friends. Our families have practically planned our wedding. They can't understand how two young adults can spend hours with each other without succumbing to our more basic instincts. The secret is simple. We simply do what is comfortable. We don't go out of our way to hold hands, but we don't shy away from it either. It would make things weird if we pretended that we found physical contact offensive. If I feel like putting my head on his shoulder, I do. If he feels like putting an arm around me, he does that as well. We love each other; we're just not in love. Nobody seems to understand the difference.

Emily shrugged. "Rhea, I think there's only two people on this planet that are in denial about you two, and the rest of us are just waiting for one of you to wake up."

I laughed.

"You just wait," she predicted. "I'm right about this. You can only fight fate for so long."

"I guess we'll see, won't we?" I challenged, and Emily smirked.

Sometimes I wished everyone would just shut up about me and Ben. All their optimism had the nasty habit of getting my hopes up.

THREE

FORTY-FIVE MINUTES later, I parked in front of Ben's house and walked in the garage entrance. I could hear the band pounding away and Ben singing one of his original songs about a girl who has broken his heart. Rachel had been this particular girl's name. I felt a twinge, remembering how she had clung to Ben like a Velcro monkey, before tucking the memory back where it belonged. Ben's wailing was hurt and angry, but in a twisted way it brought peace to my heart. Let's just say I've never been all that sad to see one of his girlfriends go.

When I entered the basement, four beautiful men smiled at me. Like any woman alive would have done, I smiled back and took a seat near Danny, the bass player, where I watched in silent appreciation as four of my best friends surrendered to their combined testosterone. When the final chord faded, I burst into applause.

"Beautiful!" I cried, as Aaron, Ben, and Danny bowed. Isaac, who was sitting at the drums, smiled and twirled a drumstick. I would give up all other men, excluding Ben, to date Isaac. At times I am convinced he feels the same way, but whenever I flirt with him, he acts completely oblivious to my advances. It's as if all of a sudden we're brother and sister.

Without further delay, Ben motioned them into their next song with a bob of his head. I had never heard it before and closed my eyes as Ben's tenor voice began the seductive ballad.

I dreamed of you again last night,
Your loving arms holding me so tight
I came awake
Only wishing to see you,
To feel you,
To touch you,
Be with you all my life . . .

As he held out the word "life," Isaac came in on the drums, and Ben's potentially beautiful ballad was transformed into a pulsing beat that had all four of them head banging. As hard as these guys tried, they never could write a ballad. I smiled and watched them bounce around with their instruments.

Ben and his band have a small following of local females, and, being a local female, I understand exactly why that is. By pure accident, they have fulfilled all of the stereotypes necessary for a boy band. Isaac is the bad boy, Aaron is the boy next door, Danny is the cerebral one, and Ben is just . . . eye candy. He looks like Scott Stapp, except with blond hair and blue eyes, which are both accentuated by his bronzed skin and flawless white teeth.

But getting back to the song.

The lyrics to Ben's new song were predictable. I was to wail about how life without male companionship was meaningless, which is amusing when you consider that I'm practically the poster girl for celibate feminism.

My eyes wandered to Ben, and I marvelled that he could be the same guy who had earned a graduate degree in computer science and had graduated with a 4.0. Countless prestigious computer companies knocked on his door, but instead, he had formed a band and started his sixth year working at UPS. I know Ben better than anyone, but some things about him are a mystery, even to me.

As the song drew to a close, I gave it a standing ovation.

"Thank you!" Ben replied as he bowed. "But you know who should be singing it."

"Oh, shut up! I'd much rather watch you guys."

Ben shook his head and lifted his guitar strap over his head. "We agree, don't we, boys?" Danny, Aaron, and Isaac nodded on cue. "It's more fun when you're with us. We'll call ourselves the Incorruptible Sandra Dees!"

The incorruptible Sandra Dee. It's been my nickname since middle school—about the time my mother died. I don't like to talk about it, but the night before she died, she asked to speak with me privately. When we were alone, she had gripped my hand.

"It's time we had a girl-to-girl talk. I've been thinking about this a long time, Rhea, and there is something I want you to promise me." I had nodded then, my young heart ready to swear to anything.

"Rhea, I don't know what your father and I did right, but you are a beautiful young girl, and I have a feeling that time is only going to make you more beautiful." I had blushed at her compliment, and she paused before continuing. "I know you don't think I understand what it's like to be your age, but I was there not too long ago, and I have a good idea of what choices lie ahead of you. And it's the choices you make in your teenage years that will define you for the rest of your life.

"Rhea, there are three things I've seen destroy a woman's life faster than anything else, and I want to warn you of these things. Number one: drugs. Promise me you won't do drugs. They will take over your life. Promise me!"

I had, squeezing her hand as she squeezed mine, neither of us knowing we would never touch like that again.

"Number two: alcohol. It will become quite the fad and

everyone will drink because the person next to them is. Promise me that you will not drink alcohol until you have graduated from college. It would kill me," she chuckled slightly (it's haunted me that she laughed when she said that. Did she have a premonition of what was to come?), "to know that one stupid night of drinking stood between you and succeeding in life. Be responsible. Wait till you're legal, at least, before experimenting with alcohol."

I promised that too, having no idea at the time how right she would be. Not drinking had indeed set me apart in social circles, and the pressure had been immense to join my peers, but I had endured.

The third promise had been delayed in coming and was phrased very carefully.

"And last: don't let boys use you." She looked me in the eye while saying this. "I've never told you this before, but your father is the only man I've ever been with. I had opportunities before your father, but not taking them was the best decision I ever made. Three of my friends became pregnant by their boyfriends, and only one of the fathers stayed around. What I'm going to ask of you will not be easy, but I hope you always remember that your mother promised you it would be worth it."

I had nodded eagerly, despite knowing what was coming.

"Rhea, save yourself for the man who will marry you. Any man will sleep with you, but only give yourself to the one who will stay with you. Will you promise to do that?"

I had promised, and that night she had died. That had been the beginning of my Sandra Dee reputation. For the longest time I hadn't told anyone of my conversation with my mother, and the person I finally told was Ben. Over the years he had actually been a great help in keeping me faithful to those promises.

And now he wanted to name his band after me and have me take over his role as lead singer. Ben, of all people, should have understood why I was declining the offer. It wasn't because I detested performing. I was declining because I loved my job too much to travel with them.

As the rest of "my men" busied themselves with their instruments, I turned to Isaac, who seemed suddenly fascinated by the structure of his drumsticks. His averted eyes offered me a few seconds to admire his sculpted arms. Isaac has the body Greek statues are patterned after and a shaved head that made him look terrifyingly tough, but all you had to do is look in his eyes to know what a sweetheart he is.

I felt bold, so I approached him.

"You're sounding good, my friend," I said, touching his arm.

"It's my drums that sound good. I just hit them," he said, trying to be modest, but not choosing the best words to do so.

"I know," I teased, my voice slightly lowered. "I saw you."

His eyes flashed up to mine. I caught a spark in them, and then it was gone.

"It really is too bad you won't sing with us," he said, looking away. "You really know how to get an audience going."

"That's nice of you to say, Isaac, but I just don't see the point of integrating myself into the band when we all know I can't go on the road."

He nodded in understanding and turned in retreat. It's the pattern of all our conversations; he says one or two sentences and then splits. I hate it.

"So, how's work going?" I asked in hopes of prolonging our conversation.

"It's all good. They're giving me benefits now."

He still wasn't making eye contact. "Really? That's great! I guess you can start injuring yourself again now, huh?"

He laughed started to say something, but then he stopped, his eyes focusing just behind me.

"Hey, Rhea," I heard Ben say as Isaac retreated. "You want

to join me upstairs for dinner? I'm sure you haven't eaten yet."

He was right. All I'd had since lunch was a bite of a feta wrap. Sometimes I think Ben knows me better than I know myself. Then it struck me how early it was, and I was surprised that band practice was over. A glance at my watch told me it was just before ten, and these boys usually played until the neighbors called to complain. The present evacuation had obviously been prearranged.

I bade the others good-bye with a confused look on my face and then turned to Ben, who was heading upstairs to the kitchen. The whole house was empty, probably for the first time since The Niners started renting it. It was unnatural.

"What's this all about?" I asked.

"All what?" he said.

I indicated the empty house . . . which seriously needed to be vacuumed. "Where is everyone?"

"I guess they had places to go."

We both knew I wouldn't buy that. "Ben, they live here. Are you saying all eight of them spontaneously went out for dinner in the middle of your sacred rehearsal time?"

"No," he finally admitted. "They left because I told them to if you said you wouldn't sing with us. And no, don't ask me how much it cost me."

I smiled. That had been my next question. "So why the big fuss?"

He looked frustrated for a moment, as if debating whether or not to divulge something he felt was important. Ultimately he relented, which was smart, considering I would have squeezed it out of him eventually.

"I've hired a manager for us, Rhea. He's good, and he's working hard on our side. He's talking about traveling, marketing, CDs, everything. He has us booked to open for some bigger bands in the next couple of months, and if they like us, we may travel with them."

"I'm not surprised. You guys are a marketing dream. So, how does this make you cancel the rest of your practice because I'm not signing on? You're already set."

Once again, he looked frustrated, only this time, I could tell he wasn't telling me the whole story. "I've let him hear some of your stuff too, and he likes it. He said you can front the band, but we have to stay consistent one way or the other. It would just be better if you came, that's all. All of us want you to. Can't you take a break from your work for a couple of months and have your stupid boss earn his own reputation for a change?"

As much as I hated going around in circles on this issue, his arguments were extremely good for my ego. My friends loved me and were going to miss me. That was good to know.

"I could, Ben, but we both know that you want this to last more than a couple of months, and I just wouldn't be happy living a life in the limelight for who knows how long."

His eyes held mine and then fell away. I had won but suddenly felt very depressed about it.

I watched as Ben turned to the fridge and pulled out a Pizza Hut box. "Want some pizza?" he asked, hurt. "I made it myself."

Uh-oh. Temper tantrum. Time for damage control. Ben doesn't know it, but it's impossible for me to be happy when he's not, and the only way to cheer myself up is to take him with me. I moved around the counter separating us and, placing my arms around his waist, leaned against his chest. He wanted to push me away, but we both knew he wouldn't.

"Aw, are you going to miss me out there on the road?" I asked sweetly.

"No," he pouted. "Not when I remember that you chose not to come."

"I know. Aren't I just so selfish?"

"Yes," he agreed, his playfulness reluctantly returning.

"And what are you going to miss the most about me?" I

expected him to answer this question sarcastically, but he surprised me by being sincere.

"I'm going to miss your smile." His arms moved around me, and one hand moved up and down my back. "I'm going to miss your work stories and our wrestling matches. I'll miss you laughing at my jokes and going on your little adventures." He paused, and his arms tightened their hold ever so slightly.

For the millionth time, I was tempted to cross one of our ever-so-fragile boundaries and see if maybe he would come with me, but then he finished his previous thought.

"I guess I'm just going to miss my little sister. It's gonna be weird without you there."

And with that zinger, Ben cemented our relationship right back where it had stalled seven years ago. I was a "little sister" to him. He might as well have just chucked my chin. In an instant, I switched from infatuated to flippant. Acting extremely happy was the only way I could disguise my disappointment.

"Well, hey! The night is young! We could do half of those things you just listed before midnight."

"I'm not in the mood to do much tonight, Rhea," he objected.

"No problem. We'll just watch a pay-per-view then, or whatever else we might find on cable."

He seemed hesitant, which was very un-Ben. Ben is Mr. Play, but talking with me that night had somehow taken the play right out of him. I grabbed his arm and dragged him after me.

"C'mon. We'll play Mystery Science Theater. You can pick the movie!"

He plodded after me like a pouty child being dragged to his room, and after two or three steps I couldn't take it any more. I whirled on him like the stern mother he was treating me like.

"What's going on with you tonight?" I asked a little more

harshly than I would have liked to.

His face read of shock, then reflection, and finally rested on insincere.

"Nothing. Let me go get the pizza so we can eat while we're watching the movie." His retreat was so fast that I was not aware of it until it was complete. From the kitchen, he waved me down the stairs.

"I'll finish warming this up and meet you down there," he said. Apparently, I was dismissed.

When he finally came down, he set the pizza box on the coffee table and sat on the opposite side of the couch, inviting weirdness between us. Distance usually means he's dating someone, but I knew for a fact that wasn't the case. It took some work, but by halfway through the movie, I was leaning against him, his arm reluctantly around me. When the movie was over, I was using his chest as a pillow and was half asleep. Then he started playing with my hair, and I was out.

Next thing I knew, the TV glowed bright blue and someone was moving me. After a moment of disorientation, I realized Ben was trying to get up without waking me, a task made impossible by my being on top of him. I gripped him and pulled him back toward me.

"Where are you going?" I muttered.

"To work," he whispered back. I had forgotten that Ben worked the sunrise shift at UPS and left for work by 2:30. It's an existence I cannot even fathom.

"I don't want you to go," I said as I snuggled in again.

"I'll quit my job if you quit yours," was his comeback.

I released him, but not before feeling him chuckle. He got up, but didn't move away. Battling curiosity, I denied the temptation to open my eyes and see what had made him pause. For a moment I romanticized that he was using the moment to watch me in innocent slumber, but then I heard the TV click off.

He had only been looking for the remote. Sometimes I

hate my wild imagination. I listened as he shuffled around, grabbing his keys from the table and a light jacket from the closet. Then with the opening and closing of a door, he was gone. Sneaking to the window, I watched him drive away, all the while trying to ignore a strange feeling in my heart that was something between a tickle and an ache. Then I gathered my things and made my own exit.

FOUR

MY MORNING routine is pretty much my personal religion. I get up between 5:00 and 5:30 and have a yogurt before I head downstairs for my daily workout. When it comes to fitness, I'm kind of a freak. I'll own it. I vary the workout from day to day, but I usually focus on combat skills and strength training.

Over the years, I've picked up a few skills. My mom always thought girls should be able to defend themselves, so she signed me up for karate when I was in elementary school. After my mom died, learning different styles of martial arts kind of became a hobby that my dad tried to balance out with dance classes and gymnastics. Now, every morning I drill tumbling skills and fighting techniques before pounding my muscles into rubber with weights. By the time I've showered, dressed, and eaten, it's usually a reasonable hour to get some work done . . . if I have a case running, which I didn't. As of last night, all my cases were closed. I was out of busy work.

Remembering my goal to design an inconspicuous handcuff key, I put on my handy leather-band bracelet. Retro as it was, I never left home without it. Kay called it my ninja bracelet since it was a veritable Swiss army knife of tools that came in handy in a pinch.

How could I make a key look benign and innocent? It would be easy to have the tool made and attached to the inside wrist for easy access. I could find some decorative way to keep it secured when I wasn't using it, but it made sense to have the whole deal professionally installed so that I wouldn't have a wardrobe malfunction at an inconvenient time and find myself helpless. I knew just the guy for the job. I stared out the window, trying to decide on design specifications, when clomping footsteps came into the kitchen.

"Good morning, Rhea."

It was Camille, Little Miss Sunshine herself. "Good morning."

"Someone got home late last night," she chided.

Normally when someone teases you about how late you were out the night before, it's a friendly, inquisitive act. Not so with Camille. She never starts any conversation that she can't end with a lecture.

"It happens," I said with a shrug.

"You'd better be careful, Rhea," she warned. "The habits you're developing are injurious to the body and the soul."

Biting my tongue, I turned and watched her retrieve a packet of oatmeal from a bowl on the counter. Camille always set up her breakfast the night before as a way to economize her time the next morning. She shook the pouch back and forth with the force of a dog snapping a rabbit's neck, tore off the top, and dumped the contents in the bowl.

"I honestly don't know how you got out of college with your health or your reputation intact," she mused. "You're so careless with both."

What do you say to that? I decided to avoid a disaster by simply nodding my head.

"Vitamin?" Camille offered, taking two large steps to hold a small pill in front of my face.

I shook my head. "Thank you for offering, but I'm okay."

"All women of child-bearing age should have 400 milligrams of folic acid a day to avoid birth defects and mental retardation in their children. You need to start taking supplements, Rhea."

I did take supplements—freakishly expensive and personally catered supplements—but if I argued that to Camille, she would simply respond as to why hers still were better than mine. She still held the pill in my face, so I had to say something.

"The iron in those vitamins makes me sick to my stomach. Thank you for offering, though."

Her eyes narrowed on me. "You must have had an iron-deficient diet as a child to have such a low tolerance for it. I guess that's understandable, considering your father would have made most of your meals."

Such a flagrant insult so early in the morning caught me offguard. Who was she to judge what my father did or didn't do right after my mother died? My jaw clenched as Camille smiled sweetly.

"I'm going to hop in the shower," she chirped. "Make sure my oatmeal doesn't boil over, will you?"

And just like that, she was gone. Thank goodness! Purposefully ignoring her oatmeal, I went to get my morning paper and brought it back to the table. I was just pulling the rubber band off when my phone rang. I picked up without checking caller ID.

"Hey, Kay." Her name is Kathryn, and everyone except me is required to call her that. I get special privileges because Kay rhymes with Rhea. That, and I'm one of five people living who have seen her without makeup.

"Good morning!" Kay replied. "Did you see the paper today?"

"Just opening it."

"Check out Section B, front page. It's on the bottom. This guy named Stephan Martel making a seven-figure salary just got busted for embezzling two hundred thousand dollars. Two hundred thousand! Can you believe it? That's like me getting busted for a hundred bucks. That's not what makes this a story, though."

"This is a story?" I asked.

"You bet it is! Don't you recognize the name? This guy was a very large contributor to our dear governor's election campaign and more than that—"

The other line beeped, and an automated voice informed me that it was Elliott.

"Kay, Elliott's on the other line. Call you back?"

"Only with good news," she said, the reporter thick in her voice.

Shaking my head, I clicked over. "Hi, Elliott."

"Congratulations on last night. You have a very happy client," he said, skipping past the greetings.

"Thank you," I replied.

"Your report is thorough, and the client is certain you got the right man. Plus, he's giving you a bonus for, and I quote, 'Parading that rapist on the evening news.' I'll take my usual fee out of the base, but the bonus is all you."

A bonus? That was so not necessary, but I knew better than to argue with a rich man on a crusade to avenge his daughter. Sometimes rich people let their money say what they're not able to.

"Please relay that I wish him and his daughter the best."

"Done. Ready for another case?" Elliott was all heart.

"Of course."

He chuckled. "I thought as much, which is good, because I have a new case for you. A businessman by the name of Stephan Martel has been arrested on accounts—"

"I'm looking at the article right now."

"Good, then I'll skip to the punch line. Martel feels the police and reporters have jumped on this with only the barest of circumstantial evidence. He believes they are going to suppress redeeming evidence, and that is why he has contracted our services. He wants us to prove that it's an employee that's embezzling."

"In the boss's name?"

"Apparently there's this guy—Paul Bradley, a financial genius—who Mr. Martel believes was stealing from the company and who created the bogus expense accounts to point the finger at Martel, should anything go wrong. The IRS took it from there."

An employee stealing and giving the money to his boss? That was a new one. "Pay?" I asked.

"Fifty if you resolve it in the next week, and minus ten for each additional week. He wants results fast."

Which was why Elliott chose me for the case. I was the only one on Elliott's crew that preferred a reverse-pay scale. Rather than billing by the hour, I started out with a cap fee and lost money with every hour I logged. It kept me from dragging things out and losing focus. If I closed this case in a week, fifty grand was mine. If I took longer, my payday grew less and less desirable.

"I'm interviewing Martel later on this morning," Elliott continued. "I'll have a tape for you in the afternoon, if you want to come by."

"Sounds good." No reason not to check it out.

"Great then," he said, sounding relieved. "I've got to go, but I'll see you later."

Bidding good-bye, I hung up and dialed Kay's number. "Guess what?" I said when she picked up.

"Mr. Section B Front Page just hired you, and you're going to give me scoops?"

I laughed. "Something like that."

"You're beautiful, and I owe you lunch."

"Uh-huh. I'll see you soon, then?"

"I'm counting the hours." Kay was in reporter heaven.

AT NOON on the dot, I made my way to Elliott's. Through the window of his office, I saw an animated client telling a story that looked like it might end with "and I caught a fish 'this' big!" so I headed straight for the conference room. My heart pumped nervously as it always does when I start a new case. I was about to hear a multi-millionaire plead his defense after which I would uncover the truth. I feel a little like God that way. People may lie to me, but they cannot hide the truth from my eyes once I start looking.

The conference room was the third door on my right, and a DVD had been left for me on top of the TV. Removing the disk from its shell, I slipped it in the player and took my seat. The screen went blue for a moment while I picked up my pad of paper and one of the many Bic mechanical pencils strewn at the side of my chair. I looked up just in time for the picture to appear.

Elliott had positioned Mr. Martel just how I wanted him: in a chair, without anything or anyone obstructing me from a full-frontal view. This way I could catch all his involuntary movements. Posture, eye contact, fidgeting, bouncing legs, or the lack of any of the above can tell me a lot, not only about the person I'm looking at but sometimes about the people or situations they are describing to me.

My methods of investigation are very unscientific. I am not a veteran police officer. I don't have unlimited connections in the bad guy underworld, nor do I have a thousand drug raids under my belt, and if I were to operate as if I did, I would be eaten alive. When investigating I have to use my fortes: youth, an open mind, people skills, tons of intuition, a little beginner's luck, and Kay. Of these, the one I use the most is my understanding of people. I let them show me what they want me to see and then investigate what they're hiding. And I do this not by hiding in cars and napping pictures, but by getting right up in people's faces and making them nervous.

Other PIs don't do this. Then again, they don't get paid for speed either.

I watched as Stephan Martel shifted his weight in his seat and stole a glance at someone off-camera, probably his lawyer. From the background noise it sounded as if four-or-so people were in on the little powwow, and I made a quick note to find out exactly who those people were. Too many lawyers didn't inspire trust between two parties. Plus, my dear client didn't have the pleading eyes of a man wrongly accused. He was too tailored, too calm, too rehearsed.

I leaned forward to listen to what he had to say. Elliott's voice came from off-camera.

"Mr. Martel, thank you for agreeing to this meeting. For the record, my name is Elliott Church and your representation, Joseph Tampa, who is also present, has hired my company to investigate claims that you have been embezzling funds from your athletic supply company of Jock Stock for the past two years."

I gave an involuntary laugh as I wrote down the lawyer's name. I didn't write down the company name. I was confident I would remember that.

"Are you ready to answer a few questions?"

"Yes," Martel's baritone voice said a little too carefully for my taste.

"First of all, you are president and CEO of Jock Stock, a company that specializes in manufacturing athletic equipment, are you not?"

"Yes, I am."

"Are you the founder of this company?"

"Yes."

"And how long have you been in business?"

"Twelve years."

So far, all of Stephan Martel's answers had been clear and concise without any straying looks to his attorney.

"What is your annual salary?"

His eyes flicked to his attorney. "It depends."

"Depends on what?"

"Sales. I don't have a salary. I take a percentage."

"So last year, how much money did you claim as gross on your tax return?"

He cleared his throat and looked at his lawyer again, and I heard a non-miked voice say, "It's going to be on the news anyway, Steve."

"Fine," he said. "1.2 million."

"Before taxes?" Elliott echoed.

"Yes. Before taxes."

"And they're trying to blame you for embezzling two hundred thousand? That's ridiculous!" The line was canned. Elliott was trying to get Stephan to relax.

"I'm glad I'm not the only one who thinks so," Stephan grumbled.

"Yet someone did embezzle two hundred thousand dollars from your company in your name. Do you have any idea how?"

"In retrospect I can see many ways. I put a lot of trust in my employees, but nothing has ever seemed out of order. I guess he was smart."

"He? So is there someone you suspect?"

Martel paused, his eyes blinking several times. "Yes, it could only be one person."

"Why is that?"

"Because only one person could have done this."

"Are you saying only one person had the power and opportunity to put you in this position?"

He shifted, obviously agitated. "Not exactly."

"Do you have personal relationships with any of your staff?"

Martel held his breath for the barest of moments. "Nothing out of the ordinary. We work together."

"So you wouldn't categorize your relationship with employees as personal?"

"No," he replied and unconsciously held his breath again. Tut-tut. The man was lying.

"And of your staff, how many could have embezzled this money?" Elliott pressed.

"Maybe six or so could have, but only one of them would have. His name is Paul Bradley, and I want you to find out how he did this, because I know it was him. Do you understand, Elliott? Don't waste your time with the others. Get Paul."

"Rest assured, Paul will get my undivided attention, Steve, but you hired me to discover the truth, and that's what I'm going to do for you."

"My attorney says the case against me is pretty solid. He's going to try to defend me, but I need you to find out how I got into this position, Elliott. Paul was very smart."

"I have to ask again, Mr. Martel. Why do you think it was Paul?"

Martel huffed and looked away. "Because he's the only one who could have," he repeated.

"You said earlier that six people had means to—"

"Elliott," he interrupted, his voice carrying the threat of a man accustomed to being in charge. "Did I hire you to question me or to do what I say? I forget."

"Understood. Moving on . . . ."

I turned the page in my notebook, watching Martel adjust the sleeve of his suit as if he were angry at it. If I were the police I would have arrested him too. He was very good at looking suspicious and not nearly as good at lying. By the end of the tape, I had three pages of notes.

It was time to pay a visit to the jailhouse.

*   *   *

"You?" Stephan Martel cried, as if he could not imagine a worse thing in the world. "First, they make me stay overnight in this rat hole, and now you're telling me that Elliott works with a teenager?"

"Looking young frequently works to my benefit, Mr. Martel," I said calmly, maintaining my professionalism. "And as for Elliott, he is a businessman who makes his money by working with the best private investigators in the business, not by being one himself."

"This is a nightmare! Do you know how much I'm paying for you?"

"Yes, I do, and I plan on earning every penny of it." Martel looked to the ceiling as if imploring the heavens to tell him what he had done to deserve his present situation. I hid a smile. "Mr. Martel, I came here to try to fill in the gaps you left when Elliott interviewed you this morning."

"I didn't leave any gaps, missy. I told it how it is."

"You told things how you want them to be. Even you don't believe what you said entirely."

"I told the truth."

I looked at him, letting my knowing eyes pierce into his until he looked away.

"I'll get to the bottom of this, I promise. The question is, is that what you're asking of me?" I watched his reaction carefully. His face was stone as he stood and looked away for a moment. He blinked twice and then looked back to me.

"That's what I'm paying you for, so get on Paul and find out how he did this to me!"

Paul, Paul, Paul. The guy was a broken record. "Is there any way you can get me into your office for a couple of days, just to get a feel for who everyone is and what Mr. Bradley does? Perhaps you could tell people I'm an independent auditor looking into the accusations against you?"

He laughed, eyes flitting over me in disbelief. "Do you honestly think you can fool anyone into thinking you have a degree in accounting?"

I raised an eyebrow in warning, my voice low to cover my annoyance. "If need be."

He shook his head, laughing.

"Perhaps a temp, if that would make you more comfortable," I amended. "One coming in to help for a few days."

He hesitated, calculating eyes assessing me. "If you really think that's necessary, I can figure something out, but I'm not sure I see what the point would be."

"Well, sir, I know you're pretty fixed on the thought that Mr. Bradley is the one who has caused you all this . . . inconvenience, but the fact of the matter is that it may have been someone else, or he may not have worked alone." He all but rolled his eyes, not liking that a woman was telling him what to think when he'd already made up his mind. "Situations like the one you're presently in are very difficult to orchestrate single-handedly."

Martel stood up, signaling to the guard. "I'll give you today and tomorrow. Do what you can in that time. I'll tell people you're from our," he blinked, "Denver office."

I had learned from watching his tape that he liked to blink

or hold his breath when he lied. Was he lying now or just hesitating in picking an out-of-state office? And if he was lying, what was he lying about?

"Sounds good," I agreed, rising as well. He watched, then gave what sounded like a snort and left. No "good-bye." No "thank you for your help," but a snort. He was obviously not out to impress me.

I returned to my jeep and reviewed our discussion in my mind. It was too soon to draw conclusions, but I had the feeling that my most recent employer did not want me to learn the truth. He wanted me only to investigate Paul Bradley, leaving all other members of his company untouched. If it was as simple as that, why had he hired a private investigator? Just give the information to the cops. The end.

But when I assured him that I would find the whole truth, his response was not one of relief or hope, but rather, he made it a point to remind me that I worked for him, as if that bound me somehow.

Then there were his eyes. Too much was going on behind them. Honest people listened and responded. They did not calculate every response or become annoyed at simple questions. Guilty or not guilty, the man was hiding something.

And I needed to change my clothes.

SIX

MY ATTIRE was tactical. Skirt just a hair too short, heels an inch higher than comfortable, hair in the stereotypical library bun, and the rest of me tailored above reproach. It was time to see if I could get someone at Jock Stock to say something stupid. As if on cue, Kay called to check up on me right before I arrived.

"So, how's it going?" she said when I picked up. "You got a lead story for me yet?"

"Not yet," I said, turning onto Jock Stock's street. "I'm just going to meet the players now."

"Do you think he's guilty?"

"You know it's counterproductive to go into an investigation with preconceived notions, Kay. I've only spoken with him once."

"He's guilty!" she exclaimed triumphantly.

"I never said that," I said, checking my rearview mirror.

"No, but you always pull that 'I am not the judge, jury, and executioner' crap when you think they're guilty."

"I'm not saying he did it. I just don't like him. And he's hiding something."

"Give me an angle to work, Rhea. Something the other stations won't think of."

I laughed. "Beside the fact that he's a politically active Republican and you want to see him twitch and burn?"

"That has nothing to do with this," she said, purely for form. We both knew avoiding bias wasn't her strong suit.

Kay is the only person I know whose job takes up more of her life than mine does. Only in the breaks between REM sleep do I believe she is fully off duty. I've got to give her something or she will hound me until I crack. Besides, connections are a two-way street. I help her today, she helps me tomorrow.

"I don't have anything solid yet, Kay. I haven't even done background checks. I'll call you when I get some clues."

She huffed in impatience. "But I'm doing a live report from outside the jailhouse for the twelve o'clock news. You're saying I should just be boring?"

"I can't believe they actually kept him overnight," I mused, purposefully not responding to her question.

"Yeah. Judge Marsten refused to move him up in the pecking order. He doesn't kowtow to money like a lot of the others, but you're avoiding my question, Rhea."

I sighed. "You can say that Martel maintains that he was framed. Beyond that, just stick to the facts."

"The facts are that Martel is in jail and a trial date has yet to be set. That's a snore, Rhea, which means people are going to change the channel and I lose this story."

"Then it's not a story yet. And stop trying to get smut out of me about the client. Republican or not, I still only give you what helps his case."

She huffed in annoyance as I pulled up to the building. I don't know what I was expecting, but it sure wasn't the fortress I saw.

"Kay, I'm here. I gotta go."

"Call me the second you know something!"

"Byeee," I said, voice saccharine sweet, and hung up.

The nearest parking spot was three rows back from the

building, so I parked there and reassessed my preconceived notions from the day before.

Mr. Martel was right. If someone wanted to embezzle money from this company, two hundred thousand over a three-year period would be a very conservative amount. A building the size of four football fields had to have hundreds of millions flow through it a year, which would make two hundred thousand dollars little more than an indulgent vacation for Martel. No wonder he was so indignant.

I looked at the scratch paper where I had written all the information Martel had passed on to me through Elliott. He told his employees that my name was Hope Church, that I was from senior management in Denver, and that I had come to look over the finances in light of the accusations against him. I didn't have time to check out the facilities in Denver, but if I worked things right, I could keep things vague and be fine.

"For the next two days, your name is Hope," I reminded myself as I checked out my reflection in the rearview mirror. Convinced that I could act the part, I grabbed my phone, locked my doors behind me, and headed for the front entry, which was guarded by a dishwater blonde-haired twenty-something-year-old wearing blue eye shadow and a smile.

"How can I help you?" she asked me at the same moment the phone rang. She raised a finger indicating I should wait and answered the phone. "Jock Stock, this is Candace. How may I direct your call? . . . Oh, I'm sorry, he's unavailable. Would you like to leave a message on his voice mail? . . . Thank you." She pressed the transfer button followed by two-zero-zero and hung up.

"I'm sorry for that interruption. How can I help you?"

I flashed a courtesy smile, careful not to make it too friendly. The expression wouldn't match my bun. "Hi, I'm Hope Church, the financial advisor from the Denver office." Her eyes grew blank, and then confused, so I added, "Mr.

Martel said you would be expecting me."

Realization flashed into her eyes. "Of course, Ms. Church from Denver. How silly of me to forget!"

Her reaction made me nervous. She was too excited, almost giddy. Giddy for a financial advisor to visit? Whatever happened to just handing me a card, showing me to an office, and giving me an informal tour?

"Well, where to start? I'm sure you'll want to meet everyone, but first things first, you'll need this card to go from section to section. All the sensors are at hip level so the guys don't have to take them out of their wallets, so it might be good if you clip it to your waistband. Ugly, I know, but this is a man's world after all. That's why they call it Jock Stock."

I waited for her to breathe, which she finally did before giving a nervous laugh. "Card, card, card," she mumbled as she sifted through a drawer and finally found one. "What else?" she said. I was sure she was talking to herself, but I responded anyway.

"Maybe a tour of the facilities?" I offered.

"Exactly!" she said, pointing a finger at me. "And Jason is supposed to do that."

I smiled, but it was as fake as Candace's smile to me. I felt like I was in the Twilight Zone.

"Have a seat and I'll page him. Oh, and here's your card," she added as an afterthought.

I took it, nodding my thanks, and sat down on the small brown couch to the left of the reception desk. Browsing through some catalogs on a nearby end table, I pretended not to notice as Candace sneaked little peeks at me. My intuition told me what my rational mind already knew: something wasn't right.

I looked up as the door behind Candace opened and could not help but do a once over. He was a beautiful specimen of a man. He had dark hair, blue eyes, and a body that obviously frequented the gym. And not married. I checked his hand. Twice.

He came toward me, hand outstretched, and introduced himself.

"Hi, I'm Jason, and you must be Hope. We heard you might make a visit this week. I'm glad we finally get to meet you."

"I'm glad to be met," I replied smoothly. "I hear you're going to be giving me a tour of the facilities."

"You bet I am, and I'm sure you'll like what you see."

I left the insinuations of that statement alone as Jason motioned me in the direction from which he had just come. The security system gave a loud beep when his access card passed in front of it, and then he pulled the door open for me. The door led into a hall of windows framing a catwalk that allowed us to walk over the factory in its entirety while protecting us from the noise with soundproof glass and secured doors. Jason seemed to sense my interest in the design.

"Mr. Martel doesn't like having to walk through people every day to get to his office, so he created this walkway to the corporate offices. Everyone likes it, even the workers, and it leaves a more positive and professional feel when clients come in for a tour."

I had to agree. It was nice to have the factory noises muted, but it also made me feel like I was in a sci-fi movie and should have been wearing a space suit instead of stilettos and a skirt.

"Classy," I said, keeping things smooth. "So how long have you worked here, Mr.—"

"Please, call me Jason. I've been here about two years. Mr. Martel hired me right after I got my masters in finance. I think he liked the fact that I looked like one of his consumers." I could have sworn he gave his pecs a little flex, but it could have been my imagination. "Mr. Martel likes to work with healthy young people here, as you'll notice. He thinks it helps him stay in touch with his market. He's a very good businessman, actually."

"So I noticed. What exactly is it you do here?"

"Me and another guy named Paul are in charge of making sure we make very large profits. Our duties include everything from okaying the orders for raw material to contracting repairmen."

"The orders don't go through Martel?"

"I'm sure he sees them at some point, but he trusts us. I've never had him override something I've set. He pays me to do a good job so he can worry about other things."

"Sounds like he's a good delegator."

"He's just good at business in general." At the top of the stairs, Jason turned his hip pocket to the censor to beep us through.

"Can all the employees get in here with their cards?" I asked.

He furrowed his eyebrows as if confused by the question. "No. This is area is for authorized personnel only. If a regular employee wants to come up here, they have to go through Candace and then be escorted like you are right now."

Interesting. So I was about to meet all the power players. "Am I authorized to come up here?"

Once again he faltered. "At the moment, no. Oh, and here's Delores. Delores, this is Hope Church from our Denver office."

He was obviously trying to avoid my next question: Will I ever be granted access to the special door? I smiled at Delores and held out my hand to shake hers. Her long-nailed hands slipped into mine and gave me a limp fish.

"Oh, sure," she said, eyeing me up and down. "Great to have you. Would you like a bagel?" she offered, pointing to a bag on a glass table in the middle of the room.

"No, thank you," I said. "I've eaten."

"Mm-hmm," she replied, looking me up and down, her

dark eyes accusing me of an eating disorder. I'm skinny, but not that skinny.

"By the way," Jason added. "Delores is from Trinidad, so don't try and be PC by calling her an African-American. She hates it."

"That's right, honey," she said with a nod. "Pet peeve, you know. Jason's trying to set the world straight for me." Their eyes met, as if sharing a private joke. I merely watched and hoped they were not laughing at me.

"Anyway, continuing on with our tour, this is the VIP lobby, you might say. Important clients are led here because it's . . . well, more comfortable."

Apparently I don't make the VIP cut, I thought cattily. I threw that thought to the side and took a look around the special lobby. It was just like every hotel lobby I'd ever seen. Impersonal furniture, subdued colors—in this case browns— and a chandelier just nice enough to pass for expensive. Oh, and the bagels. Very classy.

I was just beginning to count the number of doors framing the lounge when I realized I was being watched. By six sets of eyes. They peered from doorways, from behind desks, and strayed from hallway conversations. After about one second of my staring back, the office was back to normal again. I blinked, wondering if I had imagined it as I turned back to Jason, catching his eyes drifting a little further south than they should have been.

A faint blush lit his face from being caught. "Let me show you your office and let you settle in before I drag you around. How does that sound?"

"Good," I replied and followed him to an office in the back corner. On the way, Jason made a few introductions. "Hi, this is Hope from Denver. Hope, this is Keith." "Hope, this is Amanda and Dan. Amanda, Dan, Hope is visiting us from Denver." None of the introductions seemed significant until the last. It was to a young man with glasses.

"Good morning, Paul. I don't think you've met Hope yet. She's here from out of town."

Paul shook my hand and didn't seem to care much for the introduction, but I did. I was from Denver, Denver, Denver, and then I was from out of town? Everyone else nodded knowingly at my presence, but Paul, my little suspect, breezed right past me without acknowledgement.

I needed a computer.

"And this will be your office for the next two days," Jason said as he unlocked the door to an office. The room was barren except for a chair, a desk, and a computer. I definitely felt like a VIP *now*. No matter. I had my wish. There was a computer. Next time I would have to be more specific in my wishing if I wanted something like a twirly chair or walls that weren't blindingly white.

"Can you give me a couple of minutes to get situated?" I asked, and he nodded.

"But only a minute. Then I'll be back for you." He winked and left. Running to the computer as quickly as my high heels would let me, I powered it on.

As the computer booted up, I made a mental list of all the people I had just met. Candace the secretary, Jason the sexy financial guy, Paul the unsexy financial guy, Delores the woman from Trinidad, Amanda with the nice smile, Keith who thought he was important in his designer suit, and who was the last? Dan. I needed to know each of their positions in the company.

The computer booted up, and I searched the icons for Microsoft Outlook. Pulling the program using the defaulted user of "Temporary," I clicked on the drop-down menu for addresses, searching names by city: Austin, Del Ray, and Los Angeles. That was the end of the list. No Denver. To make sure, I pulled up a web browser. It defaulted to the Jock Stock home page, and I typed in Denver. No results were found for my search.

I leaned back and considered what this meant, beside the fact that Stephan clearly considered me an idiot—and that for approximately two hours I had been just that. Pushing past the annoyance, I fought to think rationally.

I had to assume that everyone who was told I was from Denver was actually being informed that I was who I was: a private investigator. Those who didn't know Martel's code word must have been people he considered out of the loop of authority. I'd have to watch for the people who called me Denver. It meant they were on the in with Martel.

The question was, why had Martel done all this? He could have just as well let me in on the joke. What did he think he had to gain by going around me? Wasn't I working for him?

I tapped my pen against the desk and thought about that until Jason's voice interrupted me.

"Got something on your mind?" he asked.

"I guess so," I said honestly. I wasn't going to go out of my way to keep up pretenses now. The joke was on me. Ha ha. The only choice I had left was to use their conspiring to my advantage.

"Well, let's finish that tour I promised you."

After a stiff nod, I stood and followed him out the door.

SEVEN

THE FIRST day at Jock Stock at an end, I sat in my home office to review the files I'd "borrowed." I have this habit of giving nicknames to everyone involved in a case. It also helps save me from legal liabilities since people like Kay never know the real names of people I'm talking about. To keep things simple, everyone is a Bachelor or Bachelorette with numbers affixed to them in order of their initial importance to the case.

Paul was Bachelor #1 in my case for Martel. Keith was the vice president and CFO and had the most power in the company aside from Martel, so he was Bachelor #2. Candace, Queen of the Front Desk, was Bachelorette #1 because I knew she knew more than she was telling. Amanda, the left-wing feminist, earned the honor of Bachelorette #2. At first I'd wondered if Amanda had missed her calling as a politician by working at Jock Stock, but the more I watched her, the more I realized she got off by thriving in such a sexist environment. Besides, she was still young. There would be plenty of time to run for office in her future.

Jason, the suave ladies' man who had acted as my centurion all day long, was Bachelor #3. Very sly on Martel's part to assign me a spy I would instinctively want hanging around. The man was calculating, which was good to remember.

Delores from Trinidad was Bachelorette #3. I'd bet my payday she was clean. Bachelor #4 was a guy named Dan who watched me when he didn't think I would notice in a hooded, sick way that makes you want to lock up any children in the vicinity.

Those were my list of players. Seven people who had the access and ability to frame Martel and defame the company. A pretty long list for any company to have. Too long, which, again, made Martel look guilty. Most business owners wouldn't trust that many employees to have manipulative control of the books. Maybe one or two of them, but the rest were just there to point fingers in hope of casting "reasonable doubt." I rubbed my eyes, leaned back in my chair, and made a suspect list, placing Martel's employees in the order of initial suspicion.

Which one was cooking the books and sending money from fraudulent expense reports into a savings account with Martel's name on it? Who stood to benefit?

Without debate, I put Delores in the number seven spot. Amanda struck me as slot five, so I wrote her name there before I thought too hard about my reasoning. Keith had to go in slot two, simply because he was the CFO and all fraud would have to pass under his nose unnoticed. That Martel hadn't fired him already spoke volumes. Perhaps he and Martel did this together, or maybe Keith had orchestrated the whole thing in order to take control of the company. Couldn't rule out the plot twists.

Then there was Jason, the young, impressionable hench-man. I hesitated before placing his name under Keith's in the number three position, but that was where it belonged. Dan was just creepy, so I put his name above Amanda's in the number four spot for no reason whatsoever. The guy was guilty of something, embezzling or not.

That left Candace, the personal assistant/secretary. She was a tough one. A lot of information passed through her hands every day, and for someone of her low position, she sure did call a lot of shots. Or at least she was the mouthpiece through which many received instructions. Martel trusted her to execute his commands. Did he trust her with more? I kicked Amanda's name down a slot and wrote Candace's name in number five.

Realization hit me and I laughed. I had been hired to investigate Paul, and he was the last one on my list. That's estrogen for you. I'd mentally reserved the number one slot for Martel but had to put Paul there because the money said I had to. Besides, if Martel was guilty, he didn't do it alone. He'd worked with one of the seven people on my list and once I found who he worked with, I would find the link back to him.

My list, in order of suspicion, now read: Paul, Keith, Jason, Dan, Candace, Amanda, and Delores. It kind of irked me that the three women in the company were all on the bottom of my list based on first impressions. It made me feel like I was underestimating them based on their gender, but I let the list stand as it was.

It was only now that I had met the players that I felt comfortable running background checks. Ah, yes. One of the many joys of private investigating: printing reams of personal information about people. Thanks to private eye logins, I can point and click my way into anyone's life. Pulling up my web browser, I moved alphabetically through the names, Candace Anderson being the first.

Thirty minutes later I had a rough take on her. She reportedly grossed thirty thousand a year, which was pretty good for a receptionist. Her apartment cost her nine hundred dollars a month (without utilities), her car payment was just over three fifty, and her comprehensive insurance was more than two hundred a month. After adding that all up and subtracting taxes, a person was left to wonder how she ate during the month.

I breezed through her other information. It wasn't nearly as interesting as her income. She had an associate's degree, was born March twenty-seventh, had four speeding tickets since she was sixteen, three credit cards—

My cell phone rang and I answered it before the first ring could finish. Of course it was Kay. It was always Kay whenever I started a case like this. "How did your noon report go?"

"Boring. How was your day at the infamous Jock Stock?"

I tapped all of Candace's printouts so they were lined up and slid them in a folder. "A joke. Martel told everyone of importance who I was, which is good, I guess, because it lets me know who is close to him."

"Are you going to tell me, or just tease me?"

I sighed. "Okay, here's the low-down." We've played this game before. I explain the case and the players in bachelor–bachelorette terms, and Kay gives me her insight. "Bachelors #2 and #3 control all the finances, and #3 says Martel rarely, if ever, double checks their work because he trusts them implicitly. #2 is quiet, but not necessarily shy, and avoided me the entire day. I guess he has a fear of PIs."

"But weren't you there as an employee?"

"Theoretically, yes. But my false identity was sabotaged by Martel. He established a little code word to let everyone he wanted to know exactly who I was and why I was there."

"Does he know you figured that out?"

"I don't believe so. You're the first person I've told out loud, although let me tell you, I was not happy."

She chuckled. "Oh, I can imagine. When are you going to talk to him again?"

"I don't know. I might be making another trip out to the jail."

"Jail?" Her voice sounded confused. "He got out on bail today. Didn't you know that?"

"What? When?" I asked, angry with myself for not

remembering to follow up on the bail hearing myself. I'd figure Elliott would call to tell me and my day at Jock Stock had completely distracted me.

"It was late afternoon. We showed a clip on the five o'clock news. I was wondering why you weren't there."

I looked at my watch. It was past eight.

"Is it, like, Keep a Secret from Rhea Day, or something?" I complained.

"I'm sorry. I thought you knew."

"Well, thanks to you, I do now. Where is he?"

"That's actually why I called you," she admitted sheepishly. "I'm camped outside his house right now. The lights are all off, and it looks like nobody's home."

"He got around you, huh?"

"Looks like it." I could see her annoyed expression in my mind. "We were hoping to get a statement from him for the ten o'clock news. We'll probably just end up using the statement from his lawyer. Boring."

In that moment, I was extremely glad I hadn't become a reporter with Kay—to be living my life in a never-ending quest for a scoop. And once you got it, the day would end, your miracle would be forgotten, and everyone would want you to provide something more amazing the next time around. Talk about frustrating. At least my roads had ends.

"Kay, I need to go. Keep in touch, okay?"

"No problem. Let me know if you find him."

"You got it."

I hung up and left my computer to pace the length of the room.

Martel was out, and no one had told me. Not even Elliott, which was inexcusable! I should have been at the hearing to witness both the allegations against him and his pleading. What was bail posted at? Who had been there to watch the proceedings? It was Elliott's policy that I witness such things, and now he wasn't even telling me about them? Anger bubbled in me, which was ultimately good, because anger makes me think much more concisely.

I whipped around and faced my computer, my peeved mind making clear connections all of a sudden.

A conniving, sexist, dishonest embezzler plus attractive, trusted, personal assistant who lives beyond her means equals what?

I moved to the desk and sifted through the papers until I found the one with her address on it. I could be there in less than twenty minutes. I needed to do something and had no other leads. No other incentive was necessary. Grabbing my keys, I headed out the door.

EIGHT

I HATE IT when people are predictable. True, it makes my job easier, but it doesn't inspire much hope in mankind when my cynical accusations pan out, and I can tell you that, at this time in my life, being a private investigator had turned me into the worst kind of cynic.

Candace lived in a colony of apartments that made me feel like I was trapped in an ant farm. The gray, stuccoed community was essentially one building with a hundred garages and people who lived above them. First, I had to find which garage door was hers and then run through the ant tunnels to find the backside of the same apartment. I was lucky she had all the lights on in the house. No one else around her did, so from there, I simply had to find a way to scale the posts supporting her balcony. Doing so was not the most graceful or painless part of my life, but I managed to do it in silence.

One look at Mr. Martel companionably doing the dishes with his trusted secretary left little doubt about who was making Candace's house payments. Their motions were so practiced that there was even less doubt that they had washed many-a-dish together before. Staying low, I slithered until I could sit under the window, and only then did I take out my Super Ear and listen.

The packaging for the Super Ear boasts that the user will

be able to hear bird calls at one hundred yards, but nowhere on the box did it say that you can hear hushed conversations through stuccoed walls. I have a more advanced listening device that costs five times what my Super Ear did, but it doesn't like walls either, so I was forced to get in close proximity if I wanted to hear conversations.

"So, your mom thinks you should quit?" Martel said.

"It doesn't matter what she says," Candace replied. "All she sees is the scandal and the headlines."

"Well, she's not alone. We've had five customers pull their business already, and it's only been one business day. Tomorrow's going to be a nightmare."

"They'll come back, Steve. Once this all blows over they'll come back for the same reasons they chose you in the first place. You've made Jock Stock the best. Scandal or not, that hasn't changed overnight."

There was a short silence during which I heard water running and dishes clanging together.

"You're too good to me. You know that, Candace?"

She laughed. "Yeah, and don't you forget it! I just can't wait to get you cleared of these ridiculous charges. I didn't like having a boyfriend who was in jail, even if it was only for one day."

Martel's tone soured considerably at that comment. "And it seems my future hangs in the hands of some teenager posing as a PI between her sorority parties. The infamous Elliott Church doesn't even run his own investigations! It's a total joke!"

"Then fire the girl and get someone else," Candace suggested easily.

Martel paused. "I would, but Elliott says she's the best and the fastest and to give her a chance."

Smiling at the praise, I almost forgave Elliott for not telling me about the hearing.

"How long are you going to give her?"

"A week, maybe."

"And then what?"

There was another pregnant pause. "I guess that depends how good she is or how good she isn't."

"Which am I?" Candace teased.

He gave a low chuckle, whispered something, and then the water flipped off and things went silent. After several seconds, I decided there was no more dialogue to be heard for the night, and removed my Super Ear.

How frustrating. I wanted to know what he meant by keeping me on the job depending on how good I was or was not. Did that mean he wanted a quick, mediocre investigation to uncover something obvious, but nothing more? Or did it mean he didn't think a woman could do what he considered a man's job? My guess was that I wasn't going to find out tonight. Martel seemed sufficiently distracted from the subject for the meantime.

For now I decided to be grateful for good timing and Kay's call. Then I tried to figure a way off the balcony.

* * *

"Wow, that is one messed up ankle, Rhea," Aaron said as he walked in The Niners' front room. "How'd you do that?"

"By playing Tarzan in the dark," I said lightly.

"She jumped off a balcony and landed on a hose," Ben clarified for me before rolling his eyes.

"Sweet!" Adam said, admiring my bulbous joint. "Were you spying again?"

Of course I was. "Maybe."

"Yeah," Ben snorted. "And now she's gong to camp out here until after curfew so she doesn't have to face interrogation by her freaky roommate."

Bingo! I had twenty-seven minutes before Camille hit the sheets. "Wouldn't you do the same?"

"I wouldn't live with her in the first place," Ben said, crinkling his nose as if he smelled something bad. "You need to give that woman her notice, Rhea."

"She's not that bad," I lied.

"Not that bad? She treats you like hired help in your own house. She bugs the crap out of me, and I don't even live with her."

"She's getting married in five months. I can wait until then."

"You know what your problem is?" Ben asked, jabbing his finger at me. "You're afraid to call people out when they cross the line."

It was hard to argue that since I wasn't quite sure where the lines people supposedly crossed were supposed to be.

"Ten bucks says that's why you hurt your ankle tonight," he said, his disgust showing through. "You spied when you could have asked. You let people walk all over you: Camille at home, Elliot at work. You do their work for them, and they get to keep the paycheck. Now here you are with a hurt ankle hiding from your roommate!"

"Well, sorry," I hissed. "I didn't know I was interrupting. I'll leave you in peace!" I wanted to stand up proudly and stomp out of his house, but my ankle screamed in pain before I could pick it up off the chair it was elevated on. I succeeded only in knocking my ice pack to the floor.

"Don't be ridiculous," Ben said as he crossed the room to replace the ice pack. "You know you're welcome here. Now stay still. Are you sure this isn't broken?"

"I didn't hear a pop."

"Did you get a head rush?" he asked, examining it.

"Yeah," Aaron cut in. "I always get a head rush when I break something."

"No, I just felt my ankle roll, and then it hurt and I couldn't walk normally."

"Keep an eye on it. Does Elliott give you insurance?"

"Life insurance," I joked. "If I die, he gets a million dollars."

It was the wrong thing to say. Ben scowled and was quiet for a moment.

"So, what was this person doing that you were spying on?"

"That's privileged information," I said lightly.

Aaron leaned forward with a mischievous gleam in his eye. "What's the nastiest thing you've seen somebody do when they don't think anyone is watching?"

"Pick their nose," I said without thinking.

"No, I'm serious!"

"I am too. It's nasty!"

He leaned back, pouting. "You're lying." He wanted more, but some stories are better left untold.

"Can we change the subject?" I asked, looking to Ben for help.

"Yes, we can," Ben replied. "So, when are you going to kick Camille out?"

"Can we change the subject?" I repeated.

"We already did. Now answer the question."

"Ben, leave it alone. The last thing a girl needs while she's planning her wedding is to find a place to live for five months."

"She could move in with her fiancé," Ben suggested.

I shook my head. "No, Camille's nothing if not proper. She won't live with him until after the wedding."

"That sucks," he grumbled. "Maybe if the loser lived with her for a day, he'd change his mind about her."

"Maybe," I agreed, immediately regretting it. Ben beamed at me in victory.

"What? Was that finally the confession I've been waiting for all this time, that you don't particularly like your overbearing roommate?"

"She and I are different, I confess, but that doesn't make her bad," I defended.

He shook his head. "Rhea, some people are just born mean, and she's one of those people. The sooner you admit that, the easier your life will be."

"Well, at least one person sees some good in her and hopes to marry her, so she can't be all bad."

Ben looked at me as if I had sprouted a new head. "You never cease to amaze me, you know that? I mean, after all that girl has done to you, you still defend her. Why?"

I shrugged. "I guess I'd rather just keep the peace."

"Well, then, you're the only one. Can't you see that Camille's just going to keep pushing and pushing until you crack?"

He was right, and I knew it. That didn't mean I had to admit it, though.

"I don't crack that easy," I said simply. Ben glared at me. Hard. He was mad at me for reasons I could not fathom, and I could see how badly he wanted to shake some sense into me, so I was surprised at the gentleness of his next words.

"Rhea, you're tired. Do you want to sleep here tonight?"

It took me a full second before I could stammer out a response. "I should go home. I have a lot to do tomorrow."

"I didn't ask if you have a lot to do tomorrow," he said patiently. "I asked if you wanted to stay here."

"No, I'll probably go home when you go to bed."

"And what if I don't go to bed?"

"Then I guess I'll stay until you go to work."

His eyes held mine for a moment and then he shook his head, frustrated again, and I realized he had just put me through a test. "Do you even have feelings, Rhea?" he asked out of the blue. "Does anything overcome your sense of duty?"

Um, was that a trick question? Because there seemed to be only one reasonable answer. "Of course!"

"Name one thing. It looks like someone inflated an inner-tube around your ankle, but you're still going to go into work tomorrow and probably act like nothing happened."

Yeah, and I would definitely have to wear slacks to pull that off. "I have a job to do."

He continued. "A job where you consistently do impossible and twisted things in the name of earning a paycheck. Seriously, who else do you know that learns how to pole dance in order to serve a subpoena or has taken a bullet for a client—"

"I was wearing a vest!" I objected.

"Completely beside the point. Can you name one other girl your age who wakes up every morning looking for an excuse for the world to lay her flat? At home you let Camille smack you around. At work you practically beg Elliott for cases that are way out of your league. Do you just not have feelings, or do you like being kicked around? I'd like to know!"

You forgot to include my masochistic relationship with you, I thought cynically. I suddenly felt very tired and let out an involuntary sigh. "Ben, could we not talk about this right now? I've had a rough day."

"Really?" he said with zero sympathy. "Tell me about it."

Touché. "You know I can't."

"Oh, that's right," he drawled. "Because of your sense of duty, right?"

"Ben, it's for other people's protection."

He placed his hand ceremoniously over his heart. "I pledge allegiance, to my duties . . . ," he began.

"Shut up, Ben."

"Fine. No problem. I'm going to bed."

"And I'm going home," I shot back.

He started to the stairs and I tried to get up, annoyed when he turned around and saw my awkwardness. He started back toward me.

"What are you doing?" I asked sharply.

"I'm going to help you up."

"I'm fine. I can get up myself. I've had years of practice."

"Shut up, Rhea. You need help. Admit it."

I shrugged his hand off my shoulder. "I'll admit that help would be convenient, but I don't need it, especially not from you!"

"Aaron, will you get me some duct tape?" he asked.

Aaron looked up from a bag of chips he had found who knows where. "Why?"

"So I have something to shut her mouth with." Then to me: "That is unless you can shut up by yourself."

I shot him the worst look I could, which covered the thrill I felt when he lifted me into his arms. Hormones don't always mesh with emotions.

"Fine," I said and pretended to be petulant as I relaxed in his arms.

He carried me outside and took me to the passenger side of my car.

"Where are your keys?" he asked.

"In my pocket, but we're on the wrong side of my car."

"No we're not. I'm driving you home."

"That's not necessary."

"Neither is going to work tomorrow, but you'll do it anyway." There was no retort for that. "Now give me your keys."

I did and even let him open the door for me. We drove in a silence that wasn't broken until he pushed the button to open my garage. When he carried me through my door, the first thing to greet us was a stream of questions from Camille about what had happened to me.

"She just rolled her ankle. No big deal," Ben replied shortly before taking me up to my bed. He tossed my keys on my nightstand and placed a haphazard kiss on the top of my head.

"Sleep tight," he said roughly.

"You too," I said, trying not to read into the situation. "Thanks for the ride. How are you going to get home?"

"I'll jog. It's only a mile."

He stood there awkwardly for a moment, and I could tell a thousand things were racing through his mind, but he finally just shrugged and headed for the door.

"Good night," he said.

"Good night," I replied and then listened to every last footstep I could until they had disappeared down the street.

FRIDAY MORNING at Jock Stock. Casual day. Apparently I'd missed the memo.

Sitting in my stark temp office, I tapped into the company server and tried to find something useful. I couldn't get onto specific computers and "drive" because they were currently being occupied. Even if I was sly, the other computers were likely to slow or freeze, and it looked like the system allowed certain files to be password protected. If anyone had stored anything helpful at all on their work computer, the human tendency would be to store it where someone needed a combination to get to it. All the files uploaded to the server were for common use and, thus, would almost certainly be useless in showing how money was being redirected creatively. I needed access to personal files, and that's all there was to that.

Leaning back, I looked at the clock. It was only ten. What I'd really needed from the beginning was after-hours access to the building so I could do things my way. Martel was right— I'd wasted my time coming in, except that now I had faces for each name. Yippee. It also meant that they all knew what I looked like, which could end up being a liability. Time would tell on that one.

Debating whether or not to call it a day, I tried to keep the limp out of my walk as I made my way to the water cooler near the bathrooms to fill my water bottle up. No one watched me, even though the air was heavy with unanswered questions. Some of them I couldn't answer, like, is Jock Stock going to shut down? Can it survive this scandal? Customers made those decisions. Some of the questions I would have answers for—hopefully by next Thursday so I could collect my full payday. Not that Martel was helping me there. Not since he realized a girl, and not Elliott, would be working his case.

Taking a seat in front my computer again, I saw Jason lean inside my door.

"Hope, are you okay? You look like you're limping a little."

"Oh, I'm fine. I tripped over my vacuum yesterday. Just call me Grace." Hope, Grace, whatever would work these days.

Jason stepped in, placing a thick file on my desk. "Here's the financial report you asked for yesterday in addition to the human resources information. Delores wants it back ASAP."

"No problem. Thank you," I replied. He didn't leave.

"Can I get you some coffee or something?"

"No, I'm good. I just need to get my work done, if that's okay."

"Of course, of course. I'll let you do whatever it is you need to do. We're going to be in the conference room with Stephan for the next hour or so. He called an impromptu meeting for all of management. But later, you know, around noon, would you like to, uh, gotolunchwithme?"

The last part of his question came out as one word, and I was flattered that he was nervous to ask me out. Unfortunately, I was meeting Elliott for lunch. Jason must have sensed my imminent rejection because he quickly added.

"Or maybe you could join me tonight. We're having a dinner at Amanda's. Pretty informal. We try to get together once a month outside of the workplace."

"How nice," I said sweetly and was glad that Jason didn't

know me well enough to notice my eyes cloud over. Dinners once a month outside of the workplace? Who did that? It did give me time to watch all the players, though, and I might pick up something. I smiled.

"I'd love to. What time?"

He smiled back. "Well, the dinner's at six-thirty, so how about if I pick you up at six?"

Uh-oh. I was supposed to be from out of town—not that anyone believed that. Still, I wasn't ready to let everyone know that I knew that they knew that I was a PI. Plus I didn't want anyone knowing where I lived.

"Maybe you could pick me up at my brother's. He lives in town, and I was thinking of visiting him after work today."

"Great. I'll get his address from you before you leave."

"Okay," I said, playing coy until I couldn't stand it anymore and turned my attention to the file he'd brought in.

"Well, I've got to get to my meeting," he said with his eyes still locked on me.

"Oh, yes. Don't let me keep you."

"I'll see you soon?"

"Tonight, if not before," I replied.

"Good," he said and left, walking into the board room.

Picking up my phone, I made a call before I forgot. Ben was still at work, but I could leave a message on his phone.

"Hey, Ben, this is Rhea. I need to have someone pick me up at your house tonight for something work-related. It doesn't matter if you're there or not, but if you are, then you're my brother, okay? Thanks a ton! See you tonight. Bye."

I hung up, noting the silence that filled the lounge. Everyone was in the meeting but me, and I was just about to unofficially join in on the proceedings. Plugging in Super Ear, I listened while going through the list of marketing dollars spent. Where did Jock Stock advertise, and how? Online? Catalogs? Industry magazines? Direct marketing? With an annual advertising budget of just over two million, there was a lot of room for misdirected funds, but at first glance, all of it seemed accounted for. Every payment was directed to a legitimate company with a strong web presence, including one affiliate website that seemed catered exclusively to reviewing Jock Stock products and referring customers. My eyebrows raised a bit when I saw how much that site was making, but the numbers all added up, and it was the same contract Jock Stock had with other affiliate websites, so no red flags.

Bummer. That would have been handy if it all came down to a bogus website.

In the board room, Martel was sounding the war drums. The company would survive! His name would be cleared! No one was getting laid off as long as they kept on working like they always had. Oh, and if anyone had information as to how he'd gotten in this mess, they were to step forward. No one did and the meeting adjourned while I was turning to the payroll section of the file. Jock Stock employed eighty-seven people, all in all. This was going to be fun.

✷ ✷ ✷

At 5:45, I pulled into Ben's driveway and checked my make-up in the rearview mirror. I looked about as good as I was capable of looking. Pausing before getting out, I tried to put myself back into a social frame of mind after spending all day with numbers. Going in tonight with everyone knowing who I was and what I was doing there presented a fun little challenge. People were fun to watch when they were trying to act normal, and most weren't as good at it as the CEO and the receptionist. I had also watched Martel's few interactions with the lovely Candace at the office. Strictly business. Neither of them made a false move, and it soon became obvious that their affair was a secret to everyone but me. For once I wasn't the odd man out.

One point: me.

It was ten minutes to six when I walked up the stairs and opened Ben's door without a knock. "Anybody home?" I called, and Ben appeared at the top of the stairs holding a drink. He looked me up and down.

"Where are you going tonight? The opera?"

I smiled nervously, wondering if I'd overdressed. "No, I'm just going to dinner and was told I should dress up."

"Hmm," was his only reply. He took a sip of his drink. "So, who's coming to pick you up?"

"His name is Jason. He works at Jock Stock, the place I'm investigating."

"How old is he?"

What did that have to do with anything? "Twenty-six. He's a nice guy."

"I bet," Ben muttered, and the doorbell rang. I turned and answered it.

Dark hair slicked back, Jason stood outside smiling ear to ear and offering a single red rose. While Ben gave a short laugh, Jason looked at me, looked at my dress, and gave me the response I had been looking for.

"You look great," he said, and he meant it. You know they mean it when they say it to your body and not to your eyes. Finally, his eyes came up and he stepped forward to give me a peck on the cheek. "This is for you," he said, handing me the rose.

"Thank you," I said with a smile and nearly jumped when I heard Ben's voice directly behind me.

"You can put it in a vase in the kitchen if you'd like," he said to me.

"Good idea, Ben. I think I will." I started up the stairs, glad they could not see me grimace from the pain that shot through my still-injured ankle as I refused to favor it with a limp. Once I was in the kitchen, I heard Ben speak.

"So you're Jason, huh?"

"Yes, and you must be Hope's brother."

I froze, praying that Ben would not say something stupid like, "Hope who?" He didn't, but he almost gave me a heart attack with what he did say.

"Yes, and let me warn you. If you treat my sister as anything less than a lady I will mess you up. You understand?"

"Of course," Jason replied.

"Don't think that just because she's my sister I don't see how attractive she is. If you touch her, I'll break your fingers off."

Jason sounded aloof and poised. "I think that's Hope's decision, not yours."

"Then you think wrong. Don't think I don't see what kind of guy you are—"

"Well, the rose is set," I said, hoping they would consider my interruption accidental. "Shall we go?"

"Absolutely," Jason managed to say with a smile. I smiled back and didn't look at Ben once as I descended the stairs.

"When will you be back?" Ben asked.

"I don't know. Maybe eleven or twelve," Jason replied.

"That's a long dinner," he grumbled.

"I'll be back when I get back," I said cheerfully. "Don't wait up for me, okay?"

I relished the look on Ben's face as he watched me walk away with another man. Inside I was thinking that if Ben would only treat me the way he told others to treat me, it would be his arm I'd be hanging on right then. But he didn't, so I wasn't, and I refused to let him get in the way of me getting to know an attractive guy.

* * *

You can tell a lot about a person by looking at their home. That's why cops like search warrants so much. Walking into

Amanda's house certainly told me a lot about her.

The entry, living room, dining room, and kitchen were all visible from the entrance, and vaulted ceilings towered above us. The carpet was a kitten gray that looked freshly laid. Potted dwarf trees were scattered strategically throughout the house, all of them real and none of them cheap or local. They screamed of their owner: "I am an activist who knows the name of each of these trees and how man is endangering their existence." But what said the most of Amanda was displayed above her mantel.

The mantel place is the pivotal point of any home. You can tell a lot about a person by how they do or do not decorate it. Some people place mirrors above the mantle, others display art, family pictures, knick-knacks from a craft shop, religious icons, or souvenirs from exotic vacations. On Amanda's wall were dozens of celebrity memorabilia, and I tried to pretend I didn't notice her watching me as I looked at them.

"They're all autographed," she said, coming to my side. I noted the hint of pride in her voice. "We're selling them for charity next week."

We? Who's "we"? I wanted to ask, but didn't.

"It's quite the collection. How much do you expect to raise?" I asked, contenting myself with letting her talk about something she liked.

"Last year we raised $600,000," she said proudly. My eyes widened in surprise, but she continued before I could say anything. "I got most of them autographed myself, and a lot of celebrities will donate one-of-a-kind pictures when they know it's for charity. That raises the bidding price considerably."

My eyes had fallen on some life-size pictures of the *Dexter* cast, and I wondered where a person could tastefully hang such large pictures in their house. She must have followed the direction of my eyes because she commented on the pictures.

"Die-hards go for pictures like that, but I still try to give them a quality product for their donation. The frames are solid walnut, cherry, or other similar woods. None of the frames you see are worth less than a hundred a piece—that includes the five-by-sevens—so they're getting something for their money."

I nodded, contemplating the irony that while some trees were nurtured within the walls of her home with more care than the average human receives, she had no qualms sacrificing others for her charity shrine. I did not mention this, however, but moved my attention to the other secrets Amanda's house had to tell me.

The room smelled lemon fresh, and I had no doubt she kept it that way on a day-to-day basis. This was a woman who liked a clean environment as much as she loved her trees. I pointed to a small, very old bonsai tree sitting atop a stand-alone shelf. At first glance, I knew it cost more than some people made in a year. Always best to play dumb, though. "What kind of tree is this?"

"Don't do it!" Jason called from the dining room. "Now we'll have to hear the sermon again."

"It's not a sermon. It's history," Amanda replied indignantly and approached the tree reverently. "This is a bonsai tree. Isn't it gorgeous?"

Gorgeous wasn't exactly the word I was thinking of. Small fortune might have been more appropriate. And she had more than one. They dotted her living room like potted plants might in a typical home, and junipers framed every significant window. There were literally tens of thousands of dollars of vegetation scattered throughout the living room, and I was quite sure I was the only guest who realized it. You aren't raised by a landscaper without learning a thing or two about plants.

"They're so cute," I heard myself say. "It looks different than the one on the Karate Kid!" Was I laying it on too thick?

Amanda's sigh let me know that I wasn't. She honestly just thought I was dumb about trees, just like everyone else in the room. I'm sure I wasn't the first person to trivialize her investment.

"That's because they're a different species. This one is a Wiandi, whereas the ones in the entry were Moniques."

"They're so tiny. I think one would look so good on my office desk. Where can I get one?" I was hoping she would divulge where she bought her plants, but I guess I played too dumb, because she started talking down to me.

"You can get some good deals on the Internet. I've seen them for twenty or thirty dollars, plus shipping."

"Really?" I asked excitedly, even though mentally I was kicking myself. A tree at that price would only be three or four years old, not forty or fifty. "That cheap, huh?"

"Sometimes," she replied vaguely.

"So are the trees going up for auction, too?" I might as well have slapped her in the face. I don't think it would have offended her any less.

"No," she said. "The trees are permanent."

"Oh," I replied as if I didn't know any better, and with that, the tree conversation was over. Amanda knew what to do with people with more money than knowledge. She linked her arm into mine and led me into the dining room. "I'll have to show you the other memorabilia we're auctioning off after we've eaten. We've got some really fantastic stuff."

"I would love to see it! Oh, and I forgot to ask what you're raising money for."

"AIDS. We try to hold a fund-raiser every year."

"That's great. It must feel good to contribute to a cause like that."

She nodded, eyes somber. "We try to make sure that money goes to people who can't afford treatment. You only have to visit a hospital once to be overwhelmed with the need people are in. It's awful."

She was right. It was awful. I searched the room for

something more festive to talk about and spotted four oil paintings representing the seasons.

"Wow! Those are nice paintings. Are they going to be auctioned as well?" I asked.

"No, those stay too." Her eyes glimmered with pride. "Orloski is a personal friend. We wouldn't let go of her paintings for anything."

Again with the "we" talk. I would look that up later, I decided, while moving in for a closer look at the paintings. The most striking of the four was done in fall colors, depicting two feminine hands reaching for each other but coming up short. There were a lot of ways to interpret it, but I went out on a limb with the obvious. "I like the metaphor for autumn. The hands are supposed to be Demeter and Persephone, right?"

"You have a good eye," Amanda complimented as she moved next to me.

"It was painted with a lot of passion," I said, feeling something uncomfortable resonate within me as I searched how I knew that. Then it hit me. It perfectly depicted how I felt about my mom. I could reach out all day long but never connect with her again. I cleared my throat, bringing myself back to the moment. "It's almost like the artist lost a mother or a daughter herself."

"Indeed," Amanda said, sending me a curious look, as if she were trying to reconcile my artful insights with my tree-tard comments. Her confusion was completely merited. I was kind of being schizo in my effort to feel her out. My opinion regarding her was the same. She wasn't the embezzler.

"Are you ladies hungry?" Keith's voice said from behind me. "We've finished tossing the salad."

"Good, then I'll take the meal out of the oven," Amanda said, heading for the kitchen.

"I'm sorry we got here late without our part of the meal," Keith's wife apologized. All she needed was a tiara and I'd have thought Miss California was in the room. Calling her a trophy wife wouldn't exactly be accurate, but I wasn't thinking Keith married her for her mind, either. Standing behind her and to the side, Keith's hand lay possessively on her shoulder. Sometimes nonverbal affection like that can be endearing, but the look in Keith's eye was more like a dog watching over its bone while still trying to play nice.

The guy was territorial. Entitled. And he was with a woman who had opportunities to stray all day every day. That gave him something to prove, and men usually proved things one out of two ways. One of those ways was money.

"Your timing is perfect," Amanda said with a wave of her hand. "The oven kept the food warm just fine."

"What are we having, by the way?" Jason asked as he moved from the kitchen to my side. I had almost forgotten he existed.

"Vegetarian enchiladas," Amanda replied, and I saw her smile when the men groaned.

"Why, Amanda?" Jason moaned. "Why do you always do this to us?"

"It doesn't kill you to vary your carnivorous diet every once in while. Now help me set the table. Neither Stephan nor Candace could make it tonight, so we're just waiting for Delores and Dan, and they should be along any minute." I looked around, noticing there was no Paul. Either he wasn't invited or always declined, because no one mentioned his absence. "Jason, you know where the china is. Why don't you and Hope do the place settings?"

Hope. That was me.

"Sure," he said and turned to me with a playful grin. "I'll do the silverware if you do the plates."

"You got it," I agreed, knowing that secretly he just wanted to follow my dress around the table.

* * *

It was quarter to midnight when Jason pulled into Ben's driveway. He turned off his engine and angled his body toward me.

"I hope you had fun tonight. Going to Amanda's is always an adventure."

"I had a great time," I said, and I meant it. Hearing Keith's wife talk about the three-carat ring Keith was upgrading her to for their ten-year anniversary while doing the mental math on what she was already wearing had given me my new number one guy. Keith had seemed comfortable and proud as she gushed about him being the best man ever, but I noticed he'd never looked at me. "You work with great people."

"Yeah, I guess I lucked out that way." Jason looked away from me and peered at Ben's house. I tried to see what he was searching for but decided just to ask.

"Looking for something?"

He looked back to me, his eyes irresistible. "I want to kiss you, but I'm afraid your brother might see."

"Him?" I said through a laugh. "Don't worry about him. He's asleep by now. He has to work at three in the morning and usually goes to bed by eight or nine."

He looked back at the house uncertainly. "I've just never had a brother talk to me like that and I don't want to—"

I turned his face toward me and interrupted. "Don't want to what?"

It only took a moment for him to catch my invitation. I let him kiss me the way he wanted to, but when his hands reached in for more, I backed away.

"Thank you for a fun evening," I said an inch away from his face.

"No. Thank you."

"I guess I'll be seeing you around?"

"Most definitely," he said as he tried to move in again. I stopped him.

"Good night, Jason."

He leaned away, poorly disguising that he had been expecting more. "Good night, Hope."

Exiting the car with a little bit of flare for his benefit, I headed to my jeep in the driveway, surprised when I heard Jason's door open.

"Where are you going?" he asked.

"My jeep. I don't live here, Jason."

"Oh, yeah," he said as if he hadn't considered that before. "Well, let me take you home then."

I laughed. "I don't think that'd be a good idea. Besides, then I would be without transportation tomorrow morning."

"Can I walk you to your door, at least?"

"Sure," I agreed and slipped my hand into his for the final few steps it took to get to my driver's side door.

"I really did enjoy being with you tonight," he said. The moon was full and cast shadows across his face that made him look even more attractive than usual. There I was, standing with a gorgeous man who was looking at me as if the world revolved around me. What was I supposed to do when he came in for a final kiss? Refuse? I think not.

There was an invitation to change my mind about taking him home in his second kiss, but as seductive as he was, he couldn't have known how little of a chance he had. When his hand started sliding its way up from my waist, I stopped it.

"Good night, Jason." I said it with finality. He looked me in the eye and pulled away.

"Good night, then." And he walked away. I unlocked my door and got in, taking a deep breath when the door was shut safely behind me. I looked up at the house, knowing full well that I had lied to Jason. Ben had been watching. I took another deep breath and wondered why that was so important to me before gunning the engine and heading home.

TEN

AT FIVE A.M. the next morning, my eyes flew open. Frames. Plants. Autographed collector's items. Original paintings. What did they add up to? Sure, Amanda sold them for charity, but how did she afford to purchase everything to begin with?

Maybe I'd written off Amanda too soon. Gut feelings were good and all, but I couldn't cite intuition for a reason for leaving a major stone unturned. After all, it was just as easy to invest in art off the radar than it was to buy extravagant amounts of jewelry.

After my morning workout, I hit the phones and called the East Coast just to make sure stores were open.

"Potter's Frames," an unenthusiastic voice greeted me from somewhere in Boston.

"Yes, I was wondering what your pricing range is for walnut frames."

"We don't have solid walnut frames, only walnut finished frames." Thank you, Eeyore.

I'd expect this answer from a chain store, but I'd called a framing shop that claimed to be in its sixtieth year of business. How exclusive were these frames? "What if I want a solid walnut frame?"

"Good luck."

He wasn't being very helpful.

"Do you know of any shops that could make me a solid walnut frame, or maybe a cherry wood frame?"

"Nope."

I wanted to hang up, but managed to be civil. Kind of. "Well, thank you for all your help."

"No problem," he said and then hung up. I looked at the phone and shrugged. Oh, well. He was Mr. Potter's problem, not mine anymore. I dialed the next number. It took me four more shops and eager sales people until I finally got one who could speak knowledgeably.

"I could order walnut in for you, ma'am, but the final price will be triple or quadruple the price of a synthetic frame."

"What price range are we looking at?"

"For a four-foot by six-foot frame? A regular frame made of synthetic material would cost you $1,500 to $2,500. Your math is as good as mine from there, ma'am. It all depends on the grade of the wood. Do you want me to special order it for you?"

"I'll hold off for now. I need to run it past my family for a final decision," I lied.

"Well, whatever that decision is, ma'am, we can take care of you."

"I'll remember that. Thank you."

"Have a nice day!"

I hung up, moving on to a list of New York art galleries. The first number was a bust, but someone answered at art gallery number two. It was a man and it sounded as if he were speaking French. I ignored his introduction and got down to business.

"Yes, sir, I was wondering if you have ever heard of a female artist by the name of Orloski."

"Of course. She had a show with us not more than a year ago."

Was that considered recent in art time? "Do you have any of her pieces now?"

"No, I'm afraid her work is very coveted, and we never keep a piece long." Of course they didn't. He'd probably be fired if he said anything else.

"Have you heard of a series by her of the four seasons?"

"Of course." His accent sounded totally bogus now, which was endearing somehow. "It was sold not six months ago."

Not, "it was sold six months ago," but "it was sold not six months ago." "Do you recall how much it sold for?"

"Ms. Orloski's masterpiece was acquired for the sum of five hundred, I believe."

"Five hundred thousand? For the whole series?"

"Yes, ma'am. Now, if you're quite finished with my time, I believe I'll bid you a good day." The phone went dead.

Fun guy. He probably grew up in Oklahoma and had moved to the Big Apple to make his mark in the world. I loved people.

Hanging up, I looked at my list. On it were the approximate prices for three of the largest frames she had purchased for the auction pictures, a couple bonsais, and one Orloski "masterpiece." The final total was a over six hundred thousand dollars of investments for a woman who made seventy thousand a year. Ms. Amanda was now officially a suspect, unless she just happened to live with someone who was independently wealthy.

Opening my browser and signing into the county property listings, I plugged in her address and hit "enter."

My jaw dropped at the name that popped up. Not Amanda's.

I would have never picked Amanda's house as the home of a rock star, but apparently it was. And Amanda's name was listed as co-owner. It was a permanent situation, or at least it had been for the past eight years.

Amanda didn't need the money, and she'd have to be insane to jeopardize her lover's career with an embezzlement scandal when money so clearly wasn't an issue.

Amanda was off my list entirely, along with Delores and Candace, which put Keith back at the top with Paul. It was time to get a little more serious, which meant the fun was about to begin.

* * *

Saturday: Paul's day to be watched. He was the leading suspect, after all, if I were to follow Martel's instructions. Granted, I could see why Martel insisted it must be him, but if the obvious people were always the guilty ones, then society would have no need for police officers and people like me. The public could just stand around and point at people saying, "They did it!" and be right. The question was, why was Martel so positive that Paul was the man who had framed him when Keith was the one who best fit the stereotype?

I shivered in the morning breeze and rolled up my tinted window. I was using one of Elliott's cars this morning. Its windows were tinted to the degree that even if you pressed your face against the glass, you wouldn't have a clue what was inside. If a cop pulled me over, it would be an immediate ticket, but I had lucked out so far. L.A.'s good like that. People probably just assumed I was Brad Pitt or the Beckhams. I used Elliott's cars only when I was going to be parked in plain sight and couldn't afford to let anyone discover that I was playing stakeout while fielding outraged texts from Camille about Emily inviting the guys from her Gender Studies class over for a hot tub party.

After a couple of hours with zero activity, I started growing antsy. I glared at the house. There's Murphy's Law and then there's PI's Law, which states that no matter how long you sit watching the same spot, nothing monumental will occur until you drop your guard or put yourself in the most awkward position possible. All I wanted to do was get out and stretch my legs a little bit, but the moment I did would no doubt be the precise instant that my little mouse would peek out from his hole.

I took a quick survey of my surroundings. The street was dead. The only movement was the playful acrobatics of birds and the progress of what appeared to be two door-to-door salesmen who were making record time down the street as they encountered empty house after empty house. When I saw them, they were eight houses away, and I figured that if I stretched real fast I could be out and back in my car before they could hit me with their spiel.

Feeling more and more restless, I slid from my car and into the warm rays of the mid-morning sun. Knowing that if I could see him, Paul could see me, I moved a few steps down the street and leaned against a fence. I felt like a lizard on a rock and, for the first time in my professional life, I completely lost focus. All I could think of was how good it felt to stop all my running around and just enjoy one moment in the sun. In that moment there were no terrorists, no politics, no murderers or rapists, and no one that needed to pay me ridiculous amounts of money to pinpoint the problems in their lives. There were only birds chirping and an accented voice that said, "Hello, ma'am."

That was unexpected.

I furrowed my eyebrows and opened my eyes to find that the two salesmen had evidently snuck up on me. That fact pricked my pride a little bit because I was normally so aware. It then occurred to me how young they looked. The only thing that looked old about them were the ties and pressed pants they were wearing.

"My name is Elder Gonzales," the one with darker skin continued, "and this is my companion, Elder Wright."

Whoa. That was a lot of information real fast. In less than

five seconds, I had learned that they were both named Elder and that they were gay. I flashed them a courtesy smile as my eyes passed over Elder Gonzales skeptically. The guy wore a thread-bare, oversized suit that looked like it had been worn daily and not washed for at least six months.

He had some serious stepping up to do if he wanted to march in the next pride parade.

Elder Wright was up to par, though. Perfect hygiene, perfect hair, perfect smile, perfect teeth—unnaturally white. The kind of guy that you lament is batting for the other team. And together, they made a very odd couple.

"I'm happy for you both, really," I said angling for my jeep. "I hope you have a real nice life together."

Elder Gonzales looked at me as if I were speaking another language. "We're missionaries for The Church of Jesus Christ of Latter-day Saints, and we have a message we'd like to share with you."

It was obvious that English was not Elder Gonzales's first language, and I was just about to cut him off and tell them how uninterested I was when the one named Elder Wright added, "Some people call us the Mormons."

"Mormons?" I asked in surprise.

"Yeah," Elder Wright replied. "Have you heard of us?"

Every bit of experience and training I had received in my life told me to give them a non-specific answer and send them on their way, so I was taken aback when I heard myself telling them the truth.

"Yeah, in school people always asked me if I was Mormon because I didn't drink." I abstained from informing them of the disdain with which people had always asked that question and how glad I had always been to be able to say I wasn't one of "those Mormons." And now I was finally meeting Mormons for myself: two guys in ties named Elder who didn't seem at all ashamed of their sexual orientation.

"Do you know what we believe?" Elder Gonzales asked.

I shrugged. "I know you don't drink or smoke or have sex—" I stopped, suddenly confused. "Wait, you guys don't believe in having sex outside of marriage, right?"

"Yes," Gonzales said, pleased I knew anything at all.

I tried to phrase my next question tactfully. "So, how does that work with you two?"

Elder Gonzales looked confused, but Elder Wright got my drift and blushed.

"We're *traveling* companions," he clarified. "We stay together for a couple months before we move on to new places and new traveling companions."

I was even more confused. "So, do you just stay at each other's houses? When do you go to school?"

"For two years we leave our homes and put off college to serve missions for our church," Elder Wright said. "I'm from Boston and Elder Gonzales is from Argentina. We pay our own way so that we can be here and dedicate our lives to teaching the gospel."

"Two years?" I said in disbelief.

"Yes, like Elder Gonzales said before, we believe our message is very important. Have you ever heard of the Book of Mormon? It's the book we get our nickname from."

Yes, I had heard of it, but nothing good. I did the courtesy of not telling the boys this, however. In my mind I heard Ben's voice laughing at me, daring me to be straight with them.

"I might have heard a thing or two," I replied, wondering if Paul was using this time to make his move.

"We believe that it is a companion scripture to the Bible and that a person can draw closer to God by abiding by its precepts than any other book," Elder Gonzales said, as he showed me a copy. I couldn't help but notice that he was using remarkably large words for someone who spoke in broken English, but his accent did not distract me from the magnitude of his claim. This book, they claimed, could bring a person closer to God than any other book? Including the Bible? Surely, he meant to say that excluding the Bible, that it was the best book. That still sounded wrong, though, and I began to wonder how many books these boys had actually read. Elder Gonzales distracted me from my thoughts as he plowed on. "We would like to make an appointment to come to your home and explain what this book is and how it came into our possession."

I eyed them warily. "How old did you say you guys are?"

"I am nineteen and Elder Wright is twenty."

I marveled at them. Shouldn't they be out selling drugs somewhere? For the third time, I was about to tell them to get lost when a little voice came to my head saying, *You've been accused of being a Mormon your whole life. You might as well find out why everybody thought you were one of them.*

"I don't know," I replied. "I live in Glendale and don't make a practice of inviting strangers to my house."

"We can meet you wherever you are comfortable," Elder Wright volunteered, sensing an in.

His persistence unnerved me slightly. "Look, you guys should just move on. I have a random schedule and a pretty solid track record when it comes to canceling appointments. I would be more trouble than I'm worth. Thanks for offering, though."

Elder Wright's eyes held mine in a way no man's ever had before. Here I was, wearing a bikini top and barely-there shorts, and this kid was looking into my eyes as if he saw something there that was much more interesting to him than my cleavage. I fidgeted under his gaze, despite the fact that I was feeling no discomfort. That was the problem; I was feeling quite the opposite. It wasn't physical attraction. In retrospect, I can tell you that it was the first time I felt the Spirit around another person. It was like a bubble of energy surrounded Elder Wright and me. Sure, Elder Gonzales was there too, but it was Elder

Wright who had my heart pounding.

Yet I wasn't attracted to him.

I was thoroughly confused.

He looked as if he wanted to say something, but then reconsidered. Instead he reached into his pocket and held out a business card. "This is our number. Like I said, we do this all day, every day. If you are ever interested, give us a call."

As I reached for the card, he seemed to reconsider again. He retracted the card, placed it in his book, and handed them both to me.

"Oh, I can't take your book," I protested, knowing I would never read it.

"Please, take it. I can get another. I just wish this one was in better shape." He pointed to the gold lettering on the front, half of which had rubbed away so that it read, THE OOK OF RMON. "I've been carrying that same one a while, and the sweat of my hand took off some of the lettering."

I smiled courteously as I accepted the sweat-stained book and muttered a thanks. Then, as quickly as they had come, they left. I watched them go and wondered what it was exactly that made me feel as if the air around them was charged with electricity. I looked at the book and then back to them. They were turning the corner, on their way to the next door, when I realized how long I had left Paul unobserved.

Not giving them another thought, I returned to my car, threw their book on my seat, and continued my vigil. Thirty minutes later, when the boys knocked on Paul's door, I saw Paul quickly dismiss them and smiled despite myself. What did those guys expect, after all? They were in L.A.! People don't come here to find God—they come to L.A. to *become* God. I watched them move to the next door and didn't envy them one bit.

* * *

When noon passed and there had been no movement, I

decided to call it quits and called Ben to let him know I would be stopping by for lunch. It was either that or be pressured to join Emily's hot tub party while Camille huffed about like a martyr. No thanks.

When I arrived at Ben's house, I walked in without knocking and headed up his stairs into the kitchen. He was standing by the counter making a sandwich and when I pulled up a stool, I noticed how bloodshot his eyes were.

"Someone had a rough night," I commented. He grumbled something unintelligible.

"What was that?" I asked, just to be annoying.

"Nothing," he said as he slid me a sandwich. "So, how was *work* last night?"

Oh, yes. Playing dumb to Ben's jealousy was much better than a hot tub party with strangers. "Very productive, actually. I got some good information."

"Hmm," he grunted and bit into his sandwich.

"And how was box tossing at UPS?"

"Fine. Did he go home with you?"

I blinked, wondering if I heard him correctly. "What?"

"Last night, after he dropped you off here, did he follow you home?"

My mouth fell open, shocked that Ben, of all people, would make that leap. "Don't be silly! I could never let a suspect know where I live." I took a bite of the sandwich. Peanut butter-honey-banana. Quite the combination. I didn't care. It could have been cat food and I would have eaten it. I was hungry.

"He's a suspect?" He didn't sound at all pleased, but then again, nothing about my job pleased Ben.

"Almost everyone is right now. I can't discount someone simply because . . ." I faltered at how to finish the sentence. I had walked into a verbal trap, and Ben wasn't about to let me out of it.

"Simply because of what?"

I decided to say it, if for no other reason than to spite Ben. "Simply because I'm attracted to him."

Ben looked thoughtful as he chewed in silence. I decided it was not a time to aggravate him, so I simply ate my sandwich and waited for him to speak. He did, eventually.

"There's going to be a party tonight after our gig, if you want to come. Just music, drinks, and whatever. It'll be going all night, so you can come by any time after midnight. I assume you're working, right?"

I nodded.

"Another posh dinner with your suspects?"

I shook my head. "No, I'll just be observing tonight. Trying to see what I can see and get a feel for the integrity of the people I'm investigating."

"Jason too?"

"Jason too," I affirmed.

"Ten bucks says he's slime."

"Based on what?"

His jaw flexed as his mind brought up a mental image. "He brought you a single red rose on your first date and touched you every time you were within range. He's a boundary pusher who plays the game as long as he gets his payoff. He's a player."

I realized that Ben was right. Jason had touched me a lot, and part of me was gratified that Ben had noticed. Maybe if he got jealous enough he'd actually do something himself!

"I'll take that bet, if only for the sport of it. Not because I think you are wrong." We shook on it.

"Dinner to the winner?"

"Sounds good," I agreed. So I'd end up buying Ben a meal. It was probably as close as we'd get to dating again, only I would be paying.

"So anyway, like I said, come by tonight if you can. It's going to be a madhouse."

"I will if I can, but no promises. I'm under a lot of pressure to finish this one fast."

"Aren't you always?" he grumbled.

"Yes," I agreed. Getting paid on a reverse-pay scale had that effect.

We left it at that and finished our lunches. Ben hated Elliott, and we both knew that discussing my work only led to arguments. To avoid another one, Ben pretended to read a magazine, and I watched his drooping eyes lose the battle to stay awake.

"You look tired," I said softly. "You should take a nap."

"At two o'clock I need to—"

"That gives you an hour and a half to sleep. Can you make it to bed yourself, or do you need me to escort you?"

He shook his head. "No, I've got it. I'm sorry I wasn't a better lunch host."

"Sorry? You didn't even know I was coming."

"Even so. Next time I'll try and have some real food."

"It's a deal. Now go to bed. I can let myself out."

He nodded and pushed away from the counter. "Good night, then," he said with a little salute.

"Good night," I replied and then waited to see if he would sneak a look back. He didn't.

ELEVEN

THE REST of the day was fairly boring. I will not walk you through the tedious tasks of a private investigator, but let's just say the highlight was changing the ink cartridge on my printer. By the end of the day, all of Martel's corporate employees had a file, I had all the information I was capable of getting from the bank regarding the account used for embezzling, and I was ready to explode. I don't do well when confined to small areas for long periods of time. I went for a jog, and turned my phone off. It was time for Kay to call, and I didn't have anything for her. On the contrary, she probably knew more than I did.

As if on cue, I received a text from her: *Charges against Martel have been lowered to tax evasion. Just sent the docs to your inbox.*

You'd think Elliott or Martel would be the one to fill me in, but I chose not to care as I opened the attachment on Kay's email and read the new court documents. Apparently, auditors had gone through Jock Stock's numbers and come to the same conclusion: all money was accounted for. There weren't two sets of books, no one was skimming off the top, and all debts were legitimately collected and paid. All they could nail Martel on was not claiming invested money on his tax return. A fee had been assessed, and payment was due in thirty days.

I needed to call Martel to see if I was still employed, because if he suddenly confessed to being the owner of the disputed account, then I was out of a job.

The phone rang six times, and I was expecting to go to voice mail when Martel answered his phone. "Hello, Rhea."

I couldn't read his mood in his voice. "Hi, I'm looking at the modified accusations against you and wondering what you have to say about them."

"What do you mean?" he snapped, and I heard other male voices in the background.

"I mean, do you want me to keep looking, or are you going to pay the fine and leave this?"

"You mean like my lawyers are trying to tell me to do right now?" he said, voice low and dangerous. "Let me be clear, Rhea. It's not my account. Someone has been stealing from me, and your job hasn't changed. Show me who it is, and I'll take it from there."

He hung up without another word.

So . . . I had job security. That was good. The not-as-good news was that I had been on the job two full days and still had nothing more than suspicions to work with. Usually it didn't take this long to tune in and weed out what I've been hired to find—including how the money got funneled to the savings account.

Since my home office smelled like toner, I decided to get out for a bit and get my heart pumping. This case was a lot of sitting around while I was used to a little bit more adrenaline. There's just a certain level of thrill that comes with my usual cases where I have to find ways to deliver subpoenas to men who think they're above the law, protect people who have a price on their heads, or just even leading the paparazzi on a wild goose chase while posing as a celebrity. Those were my usual cases, not this monotonous drivel. And while running of my own free will was good, it wasn't the same as being chased by an SUV that was trying to corner me or fleeing from a club after a gang realizes you just duped them.

But at least my heart was pounding when I arrived back at home. And Emily stood in the doorway looking annoyed. Had I forgotten something or was some guy just ten minutes late for a date?

"You turned your phone off," she said as I came up the walkway.

I had forgotten something. "Yeah, I was trying to avoid a call. Why?"

"Do you remember what today is?"

Apparently I didn't and said so.

"It's Saturday. We're going dancing, remember? I've been waiting for you to come home more than a half an hour."

Vague recollections of a conversation held eons ago surfaced in my mind. Dancing? Saturday? Ah, yes! It all came back to me.

"Don't tell me you forgot!" she accused.

"Give me ten minutes and I'll be ready," I said and zoomed past her before she could get in another word. It looked like I'd be getting all the distraction I could handle that night.

* * *

Clubs may have different names, different themes, and different color schemes, but essentially they're all the same when it comes down to it. They are gathering places for people who want to be noticed. Surprisingly, I'm not one of those people. I like it when I'm not noticed, when I can just observe.

By ten-thirty, I was antsy, once again being trapped in a claustrophobic environment. Questions began to run through my head. Dan made sixty grand a year, but had no savings and next to nothing in his checking account. Why? Where did all his money go? And what had Paul been doing all day in his little duplex? Was Jason really slime? What did Jason do on Saturday nights? Then there was Keith. Guilty Keith. But how did he do it?

By eleven, I couldn't take the flashing lights and sweaty bodies anymore. I pled fatigue and made a dash for my jeep, hoping that my suspects had night lives. The first stop was at Paul's, but when I saw all his lights were off I kept on driving. He probably rose and retired with the sun, and even if he didn't, there was no way for me to know where he was now.

I had better luck at Dan's. At first, his house looked as abandoned as Paul's, but as I drew closer, I could make out the definite glow of a television through his window. Feeling brave, I parked three houses down and got out of my jeep. The street Dan lived on reminded me of a set to a Disney afternoon special, only all the extras had gone home for the day, and someone had turned off all the power to the set. I could make out bicycles, tricycles, and various children's toys in each yard. People in this neighborhood trusted each other enough to leave property in the open and their lights off. Maybe they were on a neighborhood quest to conserve energy, thus leaving the street dark enough for someone like me to creep around in. I wasn't complaining.

Dan lived in a tan brick rambler, and from the street anyone could see straight into his living room. I crept up to the window and peeked in to see what he was watching, but turned away the moment that I looked.

The next thirty minutes I will edit from this story. To summarize, I discovered that Dan's pay-per-view bills came to nearly $800 a month, and that was only part of an addiction that siphoned off a large part of his salary. Dan was not a criminal. He was a man with an unfortunate habit, and after leaving his house, I officially struck him off my list of suspects.

Back in my car, I checked the time. Almost midnight. Who would be up this late? I wasn't about to go check on Candace. I already knew what I would find there. Keith was married with children, so I assumed he would be down for the night, and I already knew Amanda liked to retire early from a conversation we had while I was at her house. Besides, I couldn't get Jason off my mind. An itch of curiosity wondered what he was doing that night. I pulled out his address, and ten minutes later I was at his house.

* * *

It is so much easier to investigate rich people who live in houses instead of apartments. Casing an apartment limits you to what you can catch through a window from the street, but with houses, the opportunities are endless. For instance, in an apartment, there is no automatic garage light to tell you that the occupant of the house has come home in the past couple of minutes, like Jason's was telling me then. I love it when people have windows in their garage doors.

I parked around the corner, since Jason knew my jeep, and as I walked down the sidewalk to his house I debated the wisdom of my actions. This street wasn't nearly as dark as Dan's, and McGruff stickers warned me every step of the way that the people here were paranoid. Still, that didn't mean I couldn't walk up to his front door and pretend to knock. That was innocent enough, right? Totally innocent. And the fact that I was a pint-sized girl wouldn't hurt should I need to plead innocence later. Besides, Jason's house was begging for someone to come snooping. Once you reached the top of the porch stairs all you needed to do was reach out to touch the eve of the low-hanging roof. It would be so easy to hop up and check out the second-story windows.

I turned around, reassessing the homes across the street. They were all dark and asleep except for one nearly half a block down. Temptation won over. It seemed I would be putting McGruff to the test as I killed the porch lights framing his front door so I could hide in shadow.

Gracefully, I pulled myself up and crept silently to the first window. It was dark with drapes drawn. I moved to the second, which also had closed drapes but was not dark. I heard laughing and a playful growl.

A growl?

Curious, I realized that there was a good chance it was Jason I had just heard. Ben's bet came to mind, and I crept closer, trying to find any way to see past the curtains. There was only one crack and all it offered me was a shot of the wall. I moved my head around, trying to find a better angle, but to no avail. I could still hear the two voices, though, one male and one female . . . and the man sounded suspiciously like Jason.

Checking over my shoulder, I made sure no one had taken notice of me. So far everything looked just how I had left it. I turned back to my peep crack and kept peeking until I was rewarded the shot of two heads locked at the lips, skin, and a tiger-print bra. It was just a glance, but it was all I needed. It was Jason.

I felt a strange sensation in my chest, almost as if someone had flicked my heart with a rubber band. Was it jealousy? Anger? Hurt pride? Whatever it was, it was quickly replaced by relief that I had not allowed him to seduce me any more than he had the night before.

The night before! Were women that interchangeable to him? And to think I had felt bad for him last night, as if I owed him what he was now getting from another girl. My mother's words returned to me: *Any man will sleep with you. Save yourself for the man who will stay with you.* It was the best advice I had ever received in my life.

Silently, I climbed off the roof and headed back toward my car. I was done snooping for the night and headed for the one place where my faith in men could be restored. I was going to Ben's.

✳ ✳ ✳

I had forgotten that Ben had said there would be a party, but I heard the music pulsing from his house before I even turned the corner into his street. Ben has very tolerant neighbors, that's for sure. I made my way up the porch steps and entered the house unannounced. No one would have heard me if I knocked anyway.

I looked around, not recognizing a majority of the people, and others only vaguely. It was Isaac who first found me. He looked nervous.

"Hey, Rhea!" he yelled over the turmoil. "I thought you weren't coming tonight."

Suddenly I felt very uninvited. "Oh, I just had something I wanted to run past Ben. Then I need to leave." It was a lie, but it's what came out of my mouth.

"Oh, well, let me see if I can go get him then."

"No problem," I replied, wondering why I even tried to yell over the music. "I'll find him myself."

"No, no!" he insisted. "Stay right here. I'll go get him."

Confused, I watched as he scampered up the stairs and turned to the left. It took me a full second to realize what turning left at the top of the stairs meant. He was going into a bedroom.

Realization hit me, and this time it was more than a flick of a rubber band. It was a knife that sliced into my heart and made me lose my breath. Ben was in bed with one of his party-goers. I tried to laugh it off as I had with Jason. Good for him! It was about time he found another girl! It had almost been a month since his last. He was a healthy young man surrounded by opportunities, after all. What was to stop him?

My heart lurched, and I swallowed hard. He was just being a normal single guy. He hadn't made any vows of celibacy like I had, so he was free to do whatever he wanted, right?

Just when I thought I had myself convinced, heat began to well up behind my eyes. I was going to cry.

Letting myself out, I rushed to my jeep, making it only halfway there before I heard my name. It was Ben. I stopped and turned around to face him.

"Where are you going?" he asked. He was not wearing a shirt.

"Home." My voice was surprisingly calm. "I had a hard day, and I thought I'd come by and try to party it off, but it's probably better if I just go home and get some sleep."

"Isaac said you wanted to talk to me," he said weakly.

I waved it off. "Oh, it's nothing that can't wait until later. I'm interrupting right now. I can always talk to you tomorrow." I turned away as I said this because I didn't trust my eyes not to betray my feigned nonchalance.

"Rhea, it's not what you think!" he called after me.

I whirled around. "Don't you dare lie to me about this!" The hiss in my voice was so harsh I gave myself the chills. Not trusting myself to say anything more, I turned back toward the street just in time to conceal a tear that had somehow escaped my eye. Taking a deep breath, I reached for the door handle.

"By the way, you win our bet on Jason. I guess it takes one to know one, huh?"

My jeep roared to life, and I jammed it into gear for an uncharacteristically dramatic exit. It was unanimous. The night was a complete loss, and it was only when I slept that the tears stopped for me that night.

TWELVE

PLEASE PASS the mustard," my three year-old cousin requested, articulating each word carefully.

"Here you go," I said, handing it to her.

"Thank you," she said sweetly.

I smiled. "You're welcome."

Courtesies finished, she turned her concentration to getting the mustard on her plate.

It was Sunday, the proverbial day of rest, and after my week, I needed it. I was running on empty and was up for a little recharging, so I went to my father's house to unwind. There's just something about my dad that breathes peace, and small miracles seem to dot his everyday life. I, for example, was eating a corn dog. That's nothing short of a miracle!

Seriously, though, my father has a gift for understanding. He can read me like a picture book and make me feel as though I am on top of the world no matter what mood I come to him in. And I desperately needed that right then.

I watched my cousin daintily squeeze the mustard bottle and couldn't help but smile again.

"She's so proper," I commented to my Aunt Sarah.

"I know. You're the cutest, aren't you, Bailey?"

Bailey nodded and continued to squirt mustard on her plate.

"We're just glad you could make it today, Rhea. You're usually doing other things on Sunday." For a moment I thought she wouldn't ask, but then she did. "So, is Ben out of town or something?"

"No," I replied simply.

"Oh. So did you have a fight?"

"No."

"I'm sorry if it sounds like I'm pestering. It's just that you're usually at his place on Sundays."

"I just thought I'd spend time with my family today," I said, watching Bailey's mustard mountain grow.

"Mm-hmm," my aunt replied before following the path of my eyes. "Oh, Bailey! Do you think that's enough mustard for now?"

"No."

I bit back a laugh. She had enough mustard on her plate for all of us.

"Well, why don't you try to eat that first and then if you want more we'll give it to you. Okay?"

"No, thank you," Bailey replied sweetly.

"Bailey," Sarah warned. "Give me the mustard."

"No!" she cried, holding it against herself. Upside down.

"Oh, Bailey, you're getting it all over yourself. Here, give it to me!"

A shrill shriek filled the room as Bailey held the bottle from her mother, and I snickered behind my hand at the two of them. My aunt shot me a look. "You're not helping."

"Sorry."

"Prove it!"

I looked at Bailey and gasped, covering my mouth as if I saw something shocking. She stopped mid-shriek and regarded me quizzically.

"Oh, my gosh, Bailey! Look at your pretty dress! It's all dirty." And indeed it was. Bailey looked down, saw the mustard she had squirted on herself, and started crying.

"It's okay," I soothed. "Do you want to wash it?"

She nodded her head, still crying. I held out my hand.

"Come here. Take my hand, and we'll go change your clothes, all right? What do you want to wear?"

"My dress," she sobbed.

"Which dress?"

"Dis dress!" she said, pointing to herself and stomping her feet.

"But that dress needs to be washed so it can be pretty again." Bailey came from the womb understanding what pretty was. She loved braids, bows, lace, dresses, and anything that made her look like a princess. I had to work with that. "What about your blue dress—"

"No!"

"Or your red—"

"No!"

"What about your—"

"Nooooooo!" she shrieked.

"Wait, you haven't heard my suggestion yet. What about the new pink one I just got for you?"

"Rhea, no!" Sarah cried.

Bailey perked up at her mother's objection, a sly smile filling her face. "Okay."

"Okay, let's go," I said, and together we skipped into a guest room—one of many—that my dad kept stocked for just such an "emergency." Sarah came to watch, clearly glad to let someone else do her dirty work.

"How do you do that?" she asked.

"Do what?" I replied.

"I'm her mother. I'm the one who's supposed to be able to trick her like that."

"Ah, but she knows you as well as you know her. She hasn't had quite as much time to figure me out. Do you want to change your shoes too, Bailey?"

"Yes, please."

"Then go pick the shoes you want." I watched as she ran to her closet.

"I just don't get it," Sarah said from the doorway.

"Don't get what?" I asked, still watching Bailey.

"You. How is it possible that you are still single?"

I forced a laugh.

"I'm serious! You're as gorgeous as a movie star, you're smart, and you're great with kids. You'd be the best mom, Rhea."

"Thanks."

"Men must be blind or stupid or both."

I was relieved for the distraction when Bailey brought me her shoes. I tugged the soiled dress over her head.

"So what's going on with Ben?"

There it was. The inevitable question.

"He seems fine," I replied, helping Bailey with her pink dress.

"Seems fine? You don't know?"

I was losing patience.

"When was the last time you saw him?"

"Last night."

"Oh? Did you two go out?" she asked hopefully.

"No. He asked me to drop by a party he was having and when I did, he was in bed with someone. We didn't have much time to talk."

"Oh," was all she could think to say. Good, maybe it would shut her up for a while. I decided to push it just a little further just to make sure.

"And yes, at the time he seemed to be doing fine."

"Oh, Rhea, I'm sorry."

I nearly cried when she said that, because I was sorry too. I was sorry and broken-hearted and wished I was the same age as Bailey so I would have an excuse to bawl my little eyes out and have someone hold me and tell me it would all be okay. But I was not three, and I had learned a long time before that crying doesn't help a thing, and soft words do not fix the truth. I strained to keep my voice nonchalant when I replied.

"About what? We're not together, Sarah. We haven't been for years."

"Apparently," she murmured. "It just always seemed like there . . . well, you know. Like there was something between you two. You're so perfect together."

"We're friends, Sarah. It's not like that's a bad thing."

"No, but it could be better. Your uncle is my best friend too."

"Good," I snapped. Bailey was changed and I decided it was safer to talk to her. "Are you ready to go finish your corn dog?"

She nodded.

"Go with your mom then," I said with a little pat to her behind. "Sarah, I'm going to go out back with my dad, if you don't mind."

"Of course not," she replied. "Bailey, can you thank Rhea for helping you with your clothes?"

"Thank you."

"You're welcome. Now go finish your lunch!"

She turned and ran to the table. Sarah looked as if she wanted to stay and talk to me, but visions of mustard and pink dresses no doubt made her think twice. After opening and shutting her mouth, she followed her daughter.

In the back, my dad was discussing renovations for the yard with his brother. I didn't want to interrupt, so I sat down in a chair swing he keeps on the patio and watched a nearby weeping willow sway in the breeze until the only sound I could hear was the wind. My uncle must have gone in, because my father was alone and walking toward me.

"How's my daughter?" he asked as he sat next to me.

"Glad to be home," I replied.

He nodded and put his arm around me. I rested my head on his shoulder.

"The yard looks great, Dad."

"Your uncle wants me to put in a putting range."

"Couldn't he put it in his yard?"

"Yes, but he says the neighborhood kids will make a mess of it."

"So naturally you should mar your yard with one? Is he going to come mow it every other day?"

"Of course not, but that's not the point, Rhea."

I knew it wasn't. My dad would change his yard into a putting green simply because he loved his little brother and it was in his nature to give. In my irritated state, I had chosen to direct my frustration toward my Aunt Sarah and my uncle, and my dad had gently corrected my actions. He was like that. He did everything quietly.

"Maybe on the side of the house," I volunteered.

"Maybe," he agreed, giving me a slight hug with his arm as we fell into silence.

* * *

By the time Monday came around, I was seeing everything from a fresh perspective. The day started at five with me beating up the punching bags in my basement. By seven-thirty I was out the door. I was going to pay a surprise visit to my dear Mr. Martel.

This case was taking too long and poking way too far into my personal life. I'd cried myself to sleep because I'd let my work and personal lives overlap. Ben hooked up with girls all the time, and I always blew it off. If he hadn't called Jason out with such disgust, I would have never gotten my hopes up that Ben and I were headed in a good direction.

I needed to finish this case and leave it in the dust. Fast.

As I entered the front lobby, Candace looked at me in surprise. Not wanting to give her indication that she had authority over me, I refrained from smiling and kept my body language impersonal as I approached her desk.

"I would like to speak with Martel." It was a command, not a request. Not knowing what else to do, she picked up the phone and dialed two-zero-zero.

"Mr. Martel? The, uh . . . Denver is here . . . I don't know . . . Can I let her through? . . . Yes, sir." She hung up and clicked a button under the desk. "I assume you know where his office is."

I nodded, pushed through the door, and made my way to his office. The face I met there was not smiling.

"What are you doing here? Everyone thinks you're back in Denver. You'll blow your little cover."

"No," I replied. "You did that for me, thanks. I'm just here to ask you some questions."

He looked annoyed. Too bad. "I am a busy man—"

I interrupted him. "A busy man who is out on bail and paying me to try to prove he never should have been arrested in the first place. So tell me, why are you working against me?"

"Against you?" he protested.

"Please, Mr. Martel, as you just said, you are a busy man. Let's not waste your time or mine by talking in circles. Why did you tell all your management, excluding Paul, that I was a private investigator?"

"I don't know what you're talking about."

"Denver, Mr. Martel? One only has to look at your website to find that as far as your company is concerned, Denver doesn't exist. My question for you is, do you really want me on this case, or should we give Elliott his cut and walk away, because personally, I'm not going to deal with your crap."

I expected him to get angry, but he only frowned and turned away. "At the time I had thought Elliott would be handling the case. It took me a bit to realize that if it was you who earned Elliott his reputation, I should trust you," he said grudgingly.

"Good. Then I hope you don't mind a few questions. First up, let's start with Candace and the apartment you pay for." His mouth dropped open, but I continued before he could deny it. "It was not a very wise place to go your first day out of prison. Your affair came dangerously close to being the top story on the ten o'clock news." Or would have been if I had made one little phone call. "How long have you been with her, and how long do you think you can hide your affair from the media and the police?" I had his full attention.

"Were you following me?" He actually had the grace to sound indignant.

"No, I was playing a hunch. Seeing as how you went out of your way to conceal the fact you were out on bail from me, I was informed later that night by a third party, who also said you had disappeared. I saw that Candace's rent was more than half her salary and took a chance. So, I repeat, how long have you and Candace been in a relationship?"

He gave up. "Sixteen months." Wow. He knew it down to the month? They must be serious. "I do pay her rent, as well as her car payment, but it's not the way it looks. We really do love each other. Candace doesn't need to embezzle. All she needs to do is ask, and I'll give it to her."

"Fair enough," I said, happy that we were finally getting somewhere. "Now Dan has some personal magazine subscriptions sent here. Why?" It was obvious from the look in his eyes Mr. Martel knew exactly what I was talking about.

"Dan's mailman lives in his neighborhood, and they go to the same church," he said on a sigh. "A little over a year ago, the mailman turned Dan into the pastor and he was told to repent. He tried for a while, but ultimately just ended up changing the shipping address for his subscriptions. The magazines are concealed when they arrive, and I allow many of the others to have mail sent here, so I couldn't see any reason to forbid him from doing the same."

"Who else receives mail here?"

"Keith, Amanda—I don't know who else. Candace is the one who sorts it all."

I tucked that information away in case it might be useful later. Wanting to test his honesty, I threw out a test question. "And what about Amanda? Where does all her money come from?"

How do you know all this? his eyes seemed to ask, but he answered my question. "Amanda is in a relationship with a rather well-known celebrity. That's where her money comes from, and I'm sure that if you decide to find out who her relationship is with that you will understand our desire to remain discrete."

I nodded, agreeing.

"Besides," Martel pressed, "Amanda's too involved in politics to do something like this."

Straight answers. Hallelujah! "Is there anything else you would like to tell me about your employees?"

"Only my reasons for why I assumed it was Paul. There's no way Delores did it; Dan doesn't have enough initiative; Amanda doesn't need the money; Jason is too inexperienced; Keith has too much to lose with his family; Candace has my money already; and that leaves Paul. He's the only one with the resources and the know-how. It had to have been him."

"That makes sense," I agreed. I needed to wait until I had something before bringing up Keith. I could plant this seed however: "But you are overlooking the fact that the account in your name now holding two hundred thousand dollars was created eight months before you hired Paul."

"It was?" This was obviously news to him.

"That would mean that Paul would have had to arrange

everything before he even applied here." That stopped Martel dead, and his face whitened as if I'd sucker punched him.

"So, you're saying it was someone else?"

"Yes, I am," I replied, glad that we were finally understanding each other. "That's why it's bad that everyone knows I'm a PI."

He didn't respond, but this time it was a good silence that filled the room. When he stood again, he was all business.

"Fine, then. From now on anything you need to know, I will tell you. You will have full access to this building twenty-four-seven. Feel free to access anything you can and let me know if you need any passwords. As far as Paul goes, I still want you to investigate him. I can't believe that he's totally innocent in this." I nodded. "Come by my place tonight after eight, and I'll give you keys and an all-access card to the building. No one but you and I will know that you have it. I promise."

I nodded again, and we shook hands.

"Don't be offended, but I do need to work now. Come by as close to eight as you can tonight."

"No problem." I walked away, realizing that one of the reasons this case seemed so boring was that I wasn't actively dealing with any of the guilty people yet. If I did my job right, that was about to change.

THIRTEEN

DUE TO the fact that I was at a dead end until everyone got off work and I could get access to the building, I called my dad and asked if he needed any help. He did, or at least said he did, so I spent the morning mowing lawns.

Pulling a sharp U-turn with my mower, I mentally went over the case. In less than eight hours I would have fully authorized, unlimited access to Jock Stock. I definitely knew what to do with that. Never mind that it had the potential to be very illegal. I would be a good girl.

I flipped another U and started the next pass, my mind wandering to the one place I did not want it to go. Ben hadn't called yesterday. He always called on Sundays and tried to get me to come over because he didn't have to work the Monday morning shift. Not calling yesterday meant he wouldn't call anytime in the near future either. He never called whenever he had a new girlfriend. It was as if he didn't want them to see me or even know that I existed. Someday I would just get smart and find a boyfriend of my own. After all, what did I think was going to happen with Ben? Did I think that one day he would just wake up and realize that I was the only woman he had ever wanted and come rushing after me, full of apologies and holding out a diamond ring?

The truth was, yes, I did, but as the years rolled on, I was starting to catch the hint that he wasn't thinking that way.

I moved on to the next row and the next, all the while trying to see any way around the truth. I couldn't find one and by the time I finished the lawn, I was ready for a break. I walked to my car and checked my phone. I had missed three calls. Two were from Kay, and one was from Emily. I called Kay first.

"You've been avoiding me," she said as she picked up.

"Only because I don't have anything solid to tell you."

"I forgot to ask, did you find Martel that night?"

I was hoping she'd forgotten about that. "Yes, but it was out of sheer love that I didn't tell you."

"I could kill you! Where was he?"

"He has a lover and when you called I was going over data that indicated who that lover might be. I was right."

"And you didn't 'tag' me?" she asked, outraged. We called it "tagging" when we gave each other leg-ups in each other's careers. "That would have been perfect!"

I laughed, realizing it felt good. "See, I knew you would feel that way, and that's why I didn't tell you. The girl is considerably younger and the story would have gone all tabloid. Don't worry, Kay, in the end of all this, I'll take care of you. We just need to choose our stories."

"We? Since when are you Jimminy Cricket?"

"Since I need to be. Anyway, what has you excited enough to call me?"

"Another account has been found in Martel's name."

"Where?"

"A tiny local credit union with no functioning security cameras. Isn't that handy?" Her voice was swimming in sarcasm.

"Strategic," I replied.

"Uh-huh. What aren't you telling me?"

To tell, or not to tell . . . "I think Martel's innocent. He's keeping me on despite the dropped charges."

"Yeah, probably because he knows what's still coming down the chute!"

There was that possibility. "It's the employees."

I had her interest. "Plural?"

"Don't know yet," I confessed. "But I have my candidates."

"Nice, so slant any reports that way?"

"Or just deliver the facts," I said dryly, and we both laughed. "I have full access to the building as of tonight."

"Hmm." She didn't sound convinced yet. "That gives him a day to cover what he doesn't want you to see. What about all the little hoops he put you through?"

"I think he felt a little betrayed by Elliott and took it out on me. Apart from that, he has admitted that he was trying to protect his employees, most of whom have one or two skeletons in their closet."

"Really?" she asked as only a reporter who doubles as a tabloid writer can.

"Yes, but there's no need for those to come out unless they're guilty," I reminded her.

"I guess not," she agreed with obvious reluctance. "So how many people are you investigating?"

"Total?" I did some quick math. "Eight."

"Eight? That's a lot!"

"I'm pretty sure I've narrowed it down to three."

"What are their names?"

She was referring to the code names we would use to discuss them.

"Bachelors one through three," I replied.

"The women are clean, huh? Let's hear it for the girls."

I smiled. "Martel thinks Bachelor #1 did it. The only problem with that theory is that Bachelor #1 wasn't even hired until months after this whole thing was set into motion."

"That would kind of discount him then, wouldn't it?" Kay said, and I could tell she was writing something down.

"Theoretically, yes, but he wants me to look into him anyway."

"Who are the other possibilities?"

"Bachelor #2. He's the one with the most to lose, so let's hope he didn't do it."

Her pen was still flying. "What does he have to lose?"

"Family."

"Oh. Yeah, that's bad." In my mind I could see the wrinkle of her nose. "What about #3? What's his take?"

"He's just a jerk. It would be nice if he was guilty, but doesn't appear to live outside his means."

"Ah, the guy who kissed you in Ben's driveway?"

How did she know that? Who had she been talking to? "That would be the one," I admitted with reluctance.

"I don't know, Rhea. You say you think there's a chance that Martel's innocent, but what you just told me about the other possibilities only makes me more convinced that he's the only choice."

She was right. All evidence did point to that, but my gut begged to differ.

"As far as I'm concerned, there is a strong possibility he could have been framed."

"As far as the IRS is concerned, he's one hundred percent guilty, and he's paying up."

Of course the IRS wanted him to pay up.

"But back to the skeletons in closets you mentioned. Anything I can use for my alter ego?" When Kay couldn't sell something to the network, she donned hear alias, Kat Eatonton, and sold it to the tabloids.

I wanted to lie, but I couldn't. "One is totally juicy."

"And you'll tell me if they're guilty?"

I sighed, thinking of Amanda, confident in her innocence. Kay would have a hay-day with her secret. I prayed I was right about him before saying, "Okay, fine. If the person is guilty."

"I'm crossing my fingers. Rhea, I've got to run, but it was nice talking to you again."

Apparently I was dismissed. "Sure. Have a good news day."

"As always," she said, and we hung up. I called Emily on her cell.

"Hello?" she nearly chirped.

"Hey, Em, it's me."

"Rhea! I'm so glad you called back. You'll never guess who called me!"

"Who?" I asked, not venturing a guess. For all I knew, it was the President of the United States for how wide her social circle was.

"Isaac!"

She was right. I never would have guessed. "What did he have to say?"

"His band has a gig at Club Exile tomorrow, and he wants me to come. He said to tell you too, but he specifically said he wanted me to come!" She squealed. I sighed. Just one of the many men who prefers my roommate over me. I flirted with Isaac every day, and he has to go and ask my roommate out. Whatever.

"That's great, Em," I managed.

"It's tomorrow, ladies' night, which means there's going to be tons of men. Say you're coming!"

I was about to decline, when suddenly an idea formed in my head. "Yeah, I'll go."

Emily paused in surprise, no doubt confused by the fact that for the first time since she had known me, I had made a definite commitment.

"For real? What about babysitting, or whatever?"

"I'll say no, if it comes down to it. Count me in."

"All right! I'm going to get some other girls, and we'll make a girls' night out of it, okay?"

"Sounds good. I'll see you tonight, okay?"

"Okay, bye."

I could almost see Emily's face as she hung up. Confused, wondering if it was really me she had just been talking to. It had definitely been me. What she couldn't have known was the agenda I was beginning to sketch out for Tuesday.

FOURTEEN

I ARRIVED AT Martel's door right on schedule. By eight thirty, I was in his corporate offices and debating which office to infiltrate first. Surgical gloves on, I moved to Keith's area. I knew the least about him, but he was the most logical choice if I wanted to pick a bad guy.

I mean, c'mon! The CFO? Who could be better positioned to embezzle than the guy over all the money?

His desk was the tidy station of a family man. An 8 by 10 picture in the corner of his desk proudly displayed his hot wife, two kids, a son and a daughter, and a golden retriever. All wore tan pants and white oxford shirts—except for the dog. It looked like one of those pictures a portrait studios blows up to cover a wall to advertise how good they are.

Sitting in his chair to get his point of view on the room, I turned on the computer and looked around while it booted up. Forest green carpet, wooden walls, standard desk, and a leather swivel chair. Pretty much what you'd expect a VP's office to look like. Bending over to reach his USB drive, I plugged in the only piece of equipment I needed that night. Martel had promised me passwords tomorrow, but I didn't need them. I had the TOOL.

In truth, passwords are something to keep the lay person

off your computer. I know the movies always show big spies being stumped when the password box comes up, but that's just there to build tension while a bomb ticks down to zero or something. The truth of the matter is that there are simple and easy ways to get past any password, and the more strange and convoluted it is, the quicker TOOL will find it. I don't know which disgruntled programmer designed TOOL and sold it to Elliott, but I'm pretty sure I would kiss him if we met face-to-face, even if he looked like a woodchuck.

The program is that beautiful.

Without me doing a thing, it filled in the main login box and took me to the Keith's wallpaper as it started to scan the hard drive, making a list of all websites visited with their logins and passwords before prioritizing programs accessed and listing files accessed in order of frequency. I did nothing but wait for the pop up box to come up and say DONE before clicking OK and turning the computer off again. I could look at everything from home.

Jason came next, getting the same treatment. If he could cheat on girls, why not cheat on his boss? While TOOL worked its magic, I searched Jason's drawers, finding nothing of a personal nature. Work was work for the boy. He didn't bring his personal life to it. That, or he didn't have enough of a personality to shape a room. A look at his web history would probably tell me which was the case.

Moving to the last office on my list, I was just about to TOOL Paul when I got nervous. There was no rational reason I should have been nervous. His computer was just like everyone else's, yet I couldn't bring myself to connect my drive. An invisible voice was hollering in my head, *Don't do it! He'll know!* So I just sat there, staring at his computer and feeling as if it were staring back. Probably because it was. For all I knew, there was a camera attached to the thing or some psycho paranoid program installed that alerted his PDA if his computer was accessed.

Like I said, my methods of investigation are not scientific, which was why I backed away from Paul's computer and left his office empty handed. I'd have plenty to sift through with Keith and Jason. His computer could wait a day.

Martel was right. On a gut level, something about the guy was suspicious.

FIFTEEN

I AM CONVINCED that anyone looks like a shady person once you see where they've been online. Shady or a complete goof-off. There wasn't a planet in the galaxy where Jason would win the Most Industrious Award or where Keith would be honored as Father of the Year, but neither looked suspicious when it came to defrauding Jock Stock. Both had a reasonable amount of debt, paid their bills on time, and lived within their means, which meant no big breaks for me in my case.

At one in the morning, I called it quits for the day. Trudging to my bed, I collapsed and stared at the dark ceiling while my mind sought an easy answer that would let me put this stupid case in the past. Someone had been putting money into an account at a credit union, trying to amass a fortune off the grid. Whether by stupidity or design, they had been caught—or Martel had been in their place.

The fact that the account was in Stephan Martel's name really meant nothing. Anyone—especially a man—could take Martel's driver's license, stick a new photo on it, and open an account in that name. In this day and age, even I could probably get away with a fake ID listing me as Stephan Martel if I butched myself up a bit. It was convenient to arrest the man whose name was on the account, but until an employee or a camera could show a positive ID, it was all circumstantial. I needed to visit the credit union. Certainly the police already had, but maybe they'd share with me too.

I also needed to get to sleep since my body was going to wake up in less than four hours demanding its morning work out. Flipping off my bedside lamp, I rolled on my side and called it a night. Or would have if I didn't feel like something was watching me. Without looking, I knew what it was. It was the Mormon book. I'd gotten sick of having it stare at me in my jeep while I did surveillance, so I'd brought it in to get it out of the way.

And now those double Os that hadn't been erased by Elder Wright's hand were staring at me in bed—willing me to pick it up.

It's 1:30 a.m., I told myself. *It's time to sleep, not to start reading the Mormon Koran.*

Five minutes later, the book still beckoned me, and I gave up. Turning my light on with a frustrated groan, I reached for the little paperback and glared at it. If I was one of those people who talked to myself, I would have had words with the book then and asked it what right it had to disturb my well-deserved sleep! As it was, I simply opened it with a sigh. I was surprised when right inside the cover there was not only writing, but a picture of a young girl.

Her message read:

> My name is Amy and my brother, Andy, is the one who gave you this book. I am so proud of him for serving a mission, because I know that this book is true and that it helps us better understand God's plan for us. Joseph Smith was a prophet and there are prophets alive today. If you listen to what my brother teaches you and ask God if it's true, then He will answer your prayers.
>
> God Loves You!
>
> Emily
>
> P.S. My favorite scripture is Helaman 14:30. It's on page 403.

My first thought was, *I thought his name was Elder,* and my second was to commend this little girl on her emotional extortion. After looking at her cute little face in the picture, how could I not read her favorite scripture?

I flipped pages until I came to 403. The recommended verse was highlighted in a brilliant yellow. I read it.

> And now remember, remember, my brethren, that whosoever perisheth, perisheth unto himself; and whosoever doeth iniquity, doeth it unto himself; for behold, ye are free; ye are permitted to act for yourselves; for behold, God hath given unto you a knowledge and he hath made you free.

Aside from being the longest run-on sentence I had ever read, it was actually pretty deep. I flipped back to the picture of the little girl and wondered if she actually understood it. She didn't look like she could be any older than twelve, and she was smiling awfully big for someone who liked such an unhappy verse. Yet my curiosity and my pride were pricked. If a twelve-year-old could read, love, and understand this book, then maybe it was worth looking over.

But not then. I seriously had to get some sleep.

✳ ✳ ✳

The next morning, I was making up my schedule for the day when I received a phone call.

"Rhea?" a male voice asked softly. It took me a moment to place it.

"Mr. Martel?" I replied.

"I just thought I'd let you know that Paul called in sick today. He's never called in sick before."

"That's good to know."

"I didn't know if knowing that would help you, but I thought I'd call just in case."

"It's a very big help. Thank you."

"I've got to go," he said and hung up. I clicked my phone

off, wondering when exactly it was that I stopped feeling guilty about what I do when Mr. Martel obviously felt as if he were committing treason. I put my phone down and scribbled out the first half of my agenda. It looked like I was going to get my crack at Paul at last.

* * *

There was considerably more movement in Paul's house than there had been on Saturday. I only wished I knew what he was doing. Lucky for me his blinds were open, giving me a view of his dining room area, which looked more like a computer parts store than a food friendly environment.

I watched him. And watched. And watched, making handcuff key after handcuff key until I could do it blindfolded. Now I just needed to pick the best one to model for the new attachment to my power band.

All the while, Paul sat at his computer typing. Every couple of minutes he would pull a piece of paper out of a shoebox to his right, look over it, set it down on his left, and then begin typing again. Out of sheer boredom I started counting until I convinced myself there wasn't a point. It was then I felt the Mona Lisa eyes of that book that had somehow made it back into my car and saw my hand reach out for it.

Why not? I had nothing else pressing at the moment besides counting papers. Why not read the Mormons' book? I skimmed through all the introduction stuff, telling me it was true-true-true and turned to the first chapter. "I, Nephi, having been born of goodly parents . . ."

I read for hours, looking up once every column to check on Paul. He was still typing away, which meant I kept reading. Nephi's family left Jerusalem. Nephi went back and became the reluctant slayer of Laban so he could obtain the plates of brass, which by my accounts seemed to be a copy of the Bible. His family wandered, suffered, murmured, repented, and crossed the great oceans to a new land.

I looked up. Paul was still typing.

The population began to grow, and the children of Laman were taught to hate the Nephites. Wars followed, prophets preached, and "not a hundredth part of it could be written." Then Nephi went on an Isaiah spree and lost me. I rubbed my eyes and considered everything else I had read. I could honestly say it was nothing like I had expected it would be. I was expecting something like, 1001 Reasons to Be a Mormon and ended up with a history book—and a compelling one at that. When it cited prophets, the language was so brilliant; it was concise and accurate without a word to spare. Every word meant something, which was not something I was used to.

I reclined my seat back and began to think about what I had read. It seemed so real to me and explained so much. I had always wondered if Christianity were true, why did so few civilizations know about Christ? Why was it that only a "chosen" few who lived in the desert got to hear the word of God? Yet, according to the Book of Mormon, other civilizations knew it as well, but had ultimately rejected it and had it taken away from their theology. The parents did not teach their children, and hence the knowledge was lost. If Jesus was who he said he was and his gospel was for all people, then that made more sense than him just talking to a few thousand people in Jerusalem and hoping the word got around.

A thousand thoughts floated through my head. Thoughts concerning faith, organized religion, scriptures, God, Christ, and what roles, if any, they played in my life. I had very purposefully left all of the above out of my life, and now it seemed the most natural thing in the world to incorporate them back in.

I thought of my mom and how she had taught me to detest organized religion in all its forms, but to believe that there was something better than the present. It seemed to me that she would like the Book of Mormon. What would she say if she were here? What would her counsel be?

I wondered this because suddenly, after years of being dead, she didn't feel so far away. If I closed my eyes, I could almost believe that she was sitting next to me in the car, trying to answer the questions I was silently asking her.

Of course it was this exact moment that Paul stood up abruptly, transferred the stack of papers back into the shoebox, and after haphazardly putting the lid back on, walked out of sight. Switching gears as quickly as I could, I shoved a piece of scratch paper in the book to mark my place and put it to the side so I could put all my focus on Paul.

Two minutes later, he walked out the side door of his duplex and got into his car. Something about him seemed different, and it wasn't until he was pulling out that I realized that he wasn't wearing his glasses. And his hair had been slicked. And he wasn't half-bad looking. Why the change? The plot thickened.

Once he was gone, I was faced with a dilemma. Should I follow him or use his time away from home to browse a little? *What would Jesus do?* a little voice whispered and I quickly ignored it. The answer to that question was, *None of the above.* And that wasn't an option for me at this juncture.

A moment's deliberation had me reaching in my backseat for some necessary tools. I was going in. In broad daylight. I was an idiot. It was a good thing I had worn a spaghetti-strapped top and tight pants. If I went in with confidence, any of Paul's neighbors who saw me would most likely assume I was a new girlfriend—that is, if Paul had girlfriends.

I got out of my car, sporting a trendy little backpack that looked like an overnight bag, and casually walked up to his side door and knocked. There was no answer, of course. I tried the handle, and miracle of miracles, found it unlocked. Turning the knob, I walked into his house as if I belonged there. The first thing that hit me was the odor. I doubted the place had had a good scouring since he had moved there because it smelled like . . . everything. It was a bouquet of every unglamorous scent possible in one little room. No wonder he had called in sick! My awareness of the smell was quickly upstaged by the computer screen, however. It was on. I couldn't believe my luck! I quickly moved to the computer. Judging by the fact that Paul had left both his door unlocked and his computer on, I didn't expect him to be gone long. I would need to work fast.

Plugging in TOOL, I let it do its thing while I looked around. Paul's place hadn't seen a woman in a *long* time. The cooking range was covered in splatters and ancient macaroni dried into a permanent fixture. Dishes piled in the sink, even though there was a dishwasher, and his fridge contained condiments, two fridge packs of Coke Zero, and lunch meat. Yum.

I was not looking forward to breaking back in here and sifting through his drawers if it came to that but was glad to at least have a warning. I'd wear my usual gloves and a surgeon's mask if it came to it.

Moving back to the computer to see if TOOL was finished, I stopped when I saw a text box overlaying the box telling me it was DONE. The second box had the header of Paul Patrol with a text box to IM the sender—who in this case had opened the conversation with, *Who are you?*

Uh-oh. I stared at the question, weighing the implications of both responding and not responding and choosing the latter. Closing the box, I clicked the DONE box and disconnected TOOL, heading to my jeep and leaving the house how I'd found it. A mess.

So Paul knew someone had touched his precious computer. Good. It might make him sweat a bit, and if he started sweating, he might start making stupid decisions and make my job very, very easy. At least he would if he was guilty and somehow started embezzling from a company eight months before he got hired.

A girl can dream for easy answers.

SIXTEEN

DRIVING AWAY from Paul's, I realized something. I was being followed. Me!

Stopping by a gas station, I used filling up as an excuse to circle my jeep and check for a GPS tracker, coming up negative. Someone was following me old school, which totally irked my pride—almost as much as the realization that I hadn't picked up on my tail until I'd let him catch me doing a little breaking and entering. That was just embarrassing.

I couldn't pinpoint what had clued me in, but whatever had tripped the alarm had me on high alert all the way home. Yet I saw nothing. He probably knew I was heading home, which meant he could hang way back or even take another route to avoid being detected. I could break my pattern and try to force him onto a side street, but then he would know I was clued in and fall even farther into the shadows.

As counterintuitive as it was, I needed to act normal and reject the instinct to fall into the trap I'd just willed Paul into. He knew someone had been on his computer, which meant if he was guilty, he was about to change his pattern and show me something I needed to see. My tail would want me to do the same—freak out with the realization I was being watched and encourage me to cover my tracks in my panic, thus practically framing my work and handing it over to him with a bow.

I had to play it cool. Playing it cool meant I either went

home or to my office. I chose home, wondering if I could spot where my personal spy had been camping out without me noticing. Probably in the strip mall parking lot four blocks from my place. It covered the main entrance to my neighborhood, which also meant I needed to keep using that unless I wanted to tip the guy off. I needed him to feel safe—like I was just a dumb little valley girl he was forced to babysit.

Parking in the garage and shutting it behind me, I went in my house, wondering if it was bugged. Emily was gabbing on the phone, and I took a moment to be grateful for roommates and how their presence protected me from stunts like the one I had just pulled on Paul. I returned Emily's wave as she hung up and headed to my room. Emily wasn't far behind me.

"You don't have work today?" she asked.

"Not until later," I replied, wishing she would go away so I could start scanning my room. It didn't feel bugged, but I wanted to be sure.

Emily was all smiles. "You wanna have lunch then? I haven't eaten yet."

"Can I take a rain check?"

She put her hand on her hip and frowned. "Okay, spill it. You've been in a bad mood all week, Rhea. What's up?"

My first reaction was to brush her off and tell her to leave me alone, but I stopped myself. The reason for my bad mood was Ben, of course, but it was counterproductive to bring that up with Emily. Maybe she could help me with something else, though.

"There's this guy, and I think he's stalking me," I said helplessly, earning her full attention. Emily could relate to stalkers.

"Nuh-uh! When did this start happening?"

"Just recently. He saw me mowing with my dad, and now he follows me everywhere." And so the embellishments began, making me feel a little guilty. I should have told Emily about my job long ago. I would have if she didn't have a mouth the size of a humpback whale. She would tell everyone she had ever met—including Camille. I wasn't ready to deal with that.

"What does he look like?" she asked, referring to my alleged stalker.

"That's just it, I don't know. He just leaves me notes telling me he knows where I live and that he's watching." Or he could, if he wanted to.

"That is so sick! So you've never seen him before?"

"No, but I've felt him watching all day today. It's like everywhere I go, he's there too. But that's not possible, is it? Do you think I'm just being paranoid?" I nearly laughed at the vulnerability laced my voice. I really sounded scared. Who knows, maybe I was.

"No way. We've been studying sexual predators in my psychology class and—"

"Sexual predators?" I cried. "You don't mean that he . . . " I didn't finish the sentence, but I did almost gag. Now I was going overboard.

Her expression was the model of somberness. "It's a possibility. They say that once these guys get fixated, stalking can become a full-time preoccupation. But I wouldn't worry if I were you, Rhea. Whoever he is, you can kick his butt. All he has to do is show his face."

I couldn't help but smile. She was right. In a physical fight, I did stand a good chance. I kind of liked that about myself.

"Could you just be on the lookout for any strange guys with weird reasons for being in the neighborhood?"

"Of cou—" She stopped mid-syllable, realization filling her eyes before she cursed.

"What is it?" I asked.

"Right after you left this morning, a man came to our door selling those nasty imposter perfumes."

My heart leapt as we switched roles. I was now the interrogator. "What did he look like?"

"Too old to be going door-to-door," she said, nose wrinkling in thought. "Maybe late thirties, brown hair, and a goatee. He was wearing sunglasses, so I didn't see his eyes."

"Any distinguishing marks? How did he dress?"

"Good arms," she recalled, squeezing her soft biceps. "And he was wearing this tight black shirt that showed off his chest to waist differential."

I snapped my fingers in front of her face. "Hello? Emily? We're talking about a psycho stalker here, not the hero of a romance novel."

"Right!" she agreed, coming out of her momentary daze. "He was physically fit and had a pretty good tan. I don't remember anything weird about him, but he did kind of remind me of a bulldog, if that helps."

"How so?"

"You know, squashed face, compact build. Looked like if he were to get in a fight with a brick wall, he just might win." This said right after saying that she didn't think I had anything to worry about if I were to go hand-to-hand with him. "He was wearing brown shoes too. I didn't realize that until just now. Brown shoes with a black shirt?" She pulled a face as if to indicate that made him an even more distasteful stalker.

"How tall was he?"

"Five-eight," she said confidently after a moment of thought, and I trusted her. Emily was very particular about height when it came to guys. All-in-all, Emily had handed me a good description. If that was the guy following me, I would find him.

"If you see him again, will you let me know?" I asked, even though I knew he wouldn't show himself twice. If it was him this morning, he had done what I did at Paul's—knocked, knowing I was gone, and then improvised when a roommate showed up and let him know someone was still in the house.

So sad, too bad for him.

"Of course!" Emily agreed. "I can't believe some psycho came to our front door!"

"It's okay, Em. Nothing bad is going to happen. I'll make sure of that, okay?"

"I need a boyfriend," she said distractedly. "Then when things like this happen, he can sleep over and protect us. Why don't you tell Ben to sleep here?"

"He has a girlfriend right now," I said, knowing I needed to explain no further. Emily was familiar with Ben's patterns.

"What is his problem?" she huffed, not liking the inconvenience of him being unavailable at the moment. "You're a lot prettier than the girls he dates, and you need protection from a stalker. You'd think he could pry himself from the chick of the month and come over here and help his best friend!"

A wave of depression swept through me as I realized that he would do no such thing, if for no other reason than the fact that I wouldn't give him the opportunity. I wasn't emotionally ready to give him the chance to be my hero. "Emily, I'm not telling anyone but you about this stalker guy, okay? That includes Ben, my dad, anybody—especially not Camille! Can you keep it a secret?"

"Yeah, but as soon as they find your body in a dumpster, I'm going to the cops!"

I don't know if that was meant to be funny or not, but I laughed. "You do that," I said, and then the room fell silent.

"So, do you want to go have lunch?" she offered again, as if we hadn't just been talking about a dangerous man.

"I'd rather stay home and watch the house, if you don't mind."

"Takeout then? I'll go pick it up."

I couldn't say no to that, and five minutes later, Emily was off to pick up salads from our favorite deli. Pulling out my counter-surveillance gear, I scanned the house. It was clean, which would make sense if the perfume-imposter salesman had been my stalker. Between me, Emily, and Camille, my house was nearly always occupied. He probably hadn't had the chance to bug me yet, which means he didn't know I had Emily's description. Also, Mr. Guilty was getting nervous. All points in my favor.

Now I just needed to figure out who Mr. Guilty was. Connecting TOOL to my computer, I perused Paul's hard drive. The man may as well have handed me his hard drive with a bow and said, "Merry Christmas!" All that inputting he had been doing all morning? He had been entering in all the paid invoices from Jock Stock to his bogus affiliate marketing website.

It took a while to put all the pieces together, but when they all fell into place, I felt stupid for not seeing it before. Being in accounts payable, Paul saw all the money going out to companies that did nothing but refer sales for big kickbacks on the first sale. Wanting to get in on the action, Paul used his computer savvy to create a site of his own. Looking at the site, it seemed legitimate enough—it had reviews, pictures, and even videos. What it didn't have was traffic. None. Not even a little, which begged the question, why did it account for so many referrals?

The answer to that lay with Paul's access to the company site, where he had planted the simplest seed. On the final page, where it asked who referred you, a drop-down box let you choose Internet, friend/family, advertisement, and so on. The box defaulted to "Internet," not allowing you to choose anything else. If you pressed "submit" without filling in the blank text box below the referral box, the Jock Stock site again defaulted to fill in Paul's bogus site. Hence, on a professional level, Paul's site looked like the rock star review site that kept Jock Stock afloat. Red flags would be raised in accounts payable, which Paul headed up. And if anyone questioned the website, they would look it up to find a very credible site that looked like it was doing all it said it was doing. Until you looked up the traffic and saw the site was hitless.

Bravo, Paul!

But if he was Mr. Guilty, how had he started the ball rolling eight months before he hired on? That little hiccup was something I needed to overcome before I could write a report. All I had proved so far was that Paul had abused his position to embezzle. I hadn't proved him to be the owner of the account that had gotten Martel in trouble with the IRS.

Sometimes I hate details.

Looking at the clock and realizing it was six, I took a break on my front porch, just in time to see Camille's car pull into the driveway. I was not in the mood for her. Who was I kidding? I was *never* in the mood for her, but it would be too obvious if I left now, so I stood my ground and refused to hide in my room. I had a right not to be scared off my own front porch! I waited as she parked on the side of the house, and a few moments later, I heard her professional high heels clicking against the cement. I counted how many steps it took before she reached me. Thirty-one.

"Oh, my! What a surprise! I had almost forgotten you lived here!" she cried when she saw me—like it was her house, not mine.

"Yeah, imagine that," I said.

"I hope you don't mind, but Daniel's coming over tonight. I'm making pork chops. Can I reserve the dining room for two only?"

"Be my guest," I said. "I can't speak for Emily, of course."

"Oh, I'm sure she has something else planned tonight. What about you?"

"Nothing specific," I replied. The look she gave me was one of pity, and I wanted to smack her for it.

"Rhea, you know what your problem is?"

She knew my problems? This should be good. "I'm sure you'll enlighten me."

Her nose came up an inch. "To casualize a clinical term, you're a hanger-onner."

I hadn't been expecting that. Then again, she usually hit me out of left field. "A what?"

"You are the ultimate hanger-onner. It's sad, really. Here you are, a young girl in the prime of her life, yet you never date or do anything social. Why not? All because of some childish fantasy you have about the boy next door."

Did I mention before that Camille has a graduate degree in psychology? She does, and because of that, she thinks she knows everything and is more than happy to share her wisdom with the world—solicited or unsolicited. I tried not to listen as she blabbered on.

"Rhea, you dated the guy for six months in high school, and since then, he has shown zero interest in having a romantic relationship with you. You may be pretty, but pretty does not equal longevity in a relationship. You need to meet on an emotional, spiritual, and physical level. Take Daniel and me, for example. I had to go through my fair share of frogs to find him." She chuckled as if she were old and wise and reflecting on something experienced a lifetime ago. "But I'll tell you, he was worth it. But if I would have hung on to my first boyfriend, like you are doing, then I never would have met Daniel, and we wouldn't be getting married. Do you see?"

I saw, but I did not comment. I simply stared at the horizon.

She smiled knowingly. "You're distancing me now because you don't want to see the truth, but you heard it. Whether you like it or not, you heard it. I'm sorry that I'm your only friend who cares enough to make you face it."

Friend? Camille, my friend? I almost said something I would have regretted but held my tongue. Two wrongs would not make a right, and unlike Camille, I knew what words weren't mine to say.

"Well, thank you for your candid assessment of my love life," I said instead.

She sighed, as if to say that it was always the messenger who was shot, and walked past me, shutting the door behind her with just a little more force than the average person.

Man, I really hoped her fiancé didn't break up with her. I needed her gone.

I took a few calming breaths before turning to enter myself, casually making my way up to my room. Five minutes later, I had changed into dark running clothes and packed my backpack full of assorted necessities. I still hadn't updated my bracelet with the handcuff pick. I'd get right on that as soon as the Martel case was over, which it would be, one way or another, in the next couple of days. I could feel it. I threw the backpack in my jeep so I wouldn't have to deal with Camille and her night of pork chop romance when I came back. I might need the stuff later, but for now, I needed to run.

* * *

Running uphill is a joy I reserve for my deepest moments of self-loathing. I think it's my way of punishing myself for poor performance. That night I took the inclines, trying not to hear Camille's words echo back in my head. She was right. We both knew that, but that didn't mean I could change how I felt. I had tried dating other men, but it always felt hollow and fake. When I kissed them, I felt shame; when I flirted, I felt guilty. What kind of therapy did they have to cure me of that? If there was a proven one, I would more than happily commit myself.

Was it just as simple as moving on and meeting a guy who could take Ben's place, and then I would be cured? My plans for that night at his gig were already cemented, but maybe after that would be the best time for me to start over. For my own sake, I would send a loud message to Ben, and then he would have to put up with my boyfriends. Gradually we would grow further and further apart until our current dilemma faded away and became nothing more than a humorous memory. It was worth a try, wasn't it? I decided it was, and ironically enough, in that moment, I became single for the first time in my adult life. Emotionally, I had been married to Ben.

July credit card statement.

The thought came from so far of the blue that I stumbled, and at first I didn't understand it. Keith. His July credit card statement and bank statement don't match up. I considered that for a moment and realized I just might be right. Abruptly I turned around and began the downhill journey to home.

SEVENTEEN

SURE ENOUGH, I was right. In the June of the previous summer, the Barlow family had taken a vacation to Disneyland, and it had shown up on Keith's July credit card statement. The payment had been made in full the next month, but there was no corresponding deduction in his checking account. I checked all his other bills carefully and decided that this payment had been a one-time exception. Every other payment could be accounted for, but three thousand dollars was nothing to spit at. It didn't by any means convict Keith of embezzlement, but it did give me a lead to follow and something to report to Martel.

The poor guy had been gouged by two employees, not just one. It was a miracle his company was even afloat!

As much as Martel would hate to hear that Keith was on my suspect list next to Paul, it needed to be done. Once I put his mind on the right track, Martel might uncover something for me to build on.

I picked up my cell phone and dialed Martel's number. He didn't answer, so I tried Candace's home number.

"Hello?" she said.

"Hi, this is Denver. Is Mr. Martel there?"

"I—I think you have the wrong number," she said, but the tension in her voice told me he was there.

"Don't worry, you can give him the phone. He won't be mad."

Just then I heard the phone exchange hands.

"Yes?" Martel's voice greeted.

"I'm sorry, I wouldn't call you here unless I considered it important, sir. I'll make it fast and just say—"

"I can't understand you," he interrupted. "The phone is echoing. We must have a bad connection."

The connection sounded fine to me, and I was the one on a cell phone. Land lines don't echo when there is a bad connection. They echoed when they were bugged.

Great.

"Okay, then, sir, this can wait. Sorry to disturb you. I'll just send you an encoded message as usual. Good night." I have no idea why I added that last part. It just came out.

"Good night," he said with obvious confusion, and I clicked off my phone. Candace's phone had been tapped, which almost certainly meant that Mr. Guilty knew of the affair.

The bad news was that I still didn't know who was behind all of it. The good news was it made Martel look even more innocent—unless Martel had placed the tap on the phone to monitor his lover's calls. I quickly discounted that, though. Other personality flaws aside, Martel did not have issues with trusting people, a trait made obvious in his management style and current situation.

Feeling like a caged animal, I paced my room. It was past eight when I looked at my watch. Ben's gig didn't start until ten. If I pushed it, I had just enough time to get cozy with Keith if I snooped in my clubbing clothes.

Sounded like a plan to me.

EIGHTEEN

IT'S WEIRD to break into a house where a family lives. It made me feel all criminal. When I'm dealing with shady people, all I need to do is dress a certain way, and I have full access. Breaking in isn't really all that necessary, but there was no way I was getting into Keith's house invited.

Downstairs on the main floor, a babysitter entertained the Barlow children with a DVD while she cooked mac and cheese. Keith and his wife had been gone when I got there, but I assumed they were gone for the evening as I went through Keith's home office.

If Keith really was guilty, then he was an idiot. Embezzling to buy his family's love rather than teaching them to live on a budget that he *could* provide? The man was going to go to jail. Did he really not think he could embezzle year after year and never get caught? Clearly that's exactly what he'd been thinking. Which meant he never meant to get caught. He wanted it all, even if an innocent man had to take the fall, but he had left two massive red flags in his wake.

Red Flag #1: Keith couldn't technically afford the jewelry his wife wore, nor was the jewelry financed on a credit card.

Red Flag #2: He had paid for his Disneyland vacation with untraceable funds.

He was getting money from somewhere, and he had worked at the company long enough to set up the account in Martel's name, but where was he getting the money to put in it? And if he had set up the account under Martel's name, where was the ID that let him withdraw it again? Normally I would expect him to carry it on him, but since the situation was being actively investigated, Keith would have to be an idiot to walk around with a fake ID with Stephan Martel's name on it. That meant he was hiding it—probably at home. And if not, something in his home office should point me in the right direction.

The Mickey Mouse locks on his cabinets kept me out for all of ten seconds before I started through his files with gloved hands. I love investigating organized people. They make my job so much simpler. Like having a section just for receipts and then alphabetizing them by vendor. Only someone who works with numbers all day would compulsively organize his home files the same way, allowing me to identify all jewelry receipts in less than five minutes. After a few minutes of looking, though, I started taking receipts for all large ticket items that appeared to be paid with cash.

Keith had been very busy providing for his family.

But how?

First thing I needed to do was get Martel's lawyers to send me a copy of the account activity on the bogus "Stephan Martel" accounts to see if anything directly correlated. Disneyland? The new Bowflex? The ten-year anniversary ring? Any of it? The lawyers should be able to fax the account activity to me tomorrow morning, and if my luck was good, those records might be all I needed. To really put the nail in the coffin, though, I needed the fake ID. To put a nail in both sides of the coffin, I needed to find out how Keith had done it. Check kiting? Lapping? Kickbacks? Undercharging? I'd thought I'd checked for all that, but apparently I needed to look closer.

An invisible voice told me it was time to check out of the Barlows' home, but I fought it. I knew I was in the room where Keith had stashed his fake ID. I just needed to find the little Chinese puzzle box or whatever it was currently hiding in. Looking under everything that wasn't nailed down and in everything that opened, I still came up empty, until I came to a door that opened into the hall bathroom. Turning on the light, I checked to see how my makeup was holding out.

Pausing in front of the mirror, I took a good look at the stranger who smirked back. She could be stopped for prostitution. The black hot pants I wore were as tight as a second skin, and my top certainly left little to the imagination. I regarded my body skeptically, wondering if anyone would be tempted. I worked hard to maintain an athletic body, but knew not all men were attracted to women with more muscles than curves. That didn't mean I wasn't proud of every contour I had pounded into myself, though. With satisfaction, I sucked my stomach in and saw the barest indication of a six pack. Would guys like that as much as I did? Normally I wouldn't care, because I knew Ben liked it, but the answer to that question would be important to how the evening would play out for me.

Drawing closer, I licked my finger and wiped off a dot of mascara that had somehow strayed onto my cheek bone. I had done my makeup thick and dramatic, lining my eyes for the first time in months and glossing my lips to a shine. I had also bought some shampoo that artificially helped highlight the red in my dark hair, but in retrospect, that had probably been an unnecessary step, considering the lighting at the concert would be not be designed to bring out the subtleties of hair highlights. It would be aimed at Ben, the man I had wasted too much of my youth on.

Well, things were about to change. He wanted to play other girls and ignore me? Two could play at that game, and it was my sole objective that evening to prove that to him. If he didn't want me, I'd let him know he couldn't have me!

My cell phone buzzed, and I grabbed it.

"Hello?" I whispered, backing out of the bathroom so it wouldn't echo.

"Rhea, where are you?" Emily yelled over background music. "They've already gone on! You're going to miss it!"

"I'll be there in ten," I replied, flipping my hair in the mirror before returning the door to its closed position. I usually didn't wear it down, but tonight was special.

"Good, because we're totally outnumbered. There's a group of six guys we've hooked up with, and they're all hot!"

The heavens were smiling upon me. "On my way."

"Okay, see you soon!"

We both hung up, and I checked my watch. It was 9:35. Ben had gone on way early, which was good since Kay would call me in two hours to make sure I left the club and went back to work. I couldn't indulge too much. I might get spoiled and forget my place in this world.

Making a pass through the room to ensure all the drawers were locked, I walked back into the master bedroom, stepped out of the window, and popped the screen back into place. I'd chosen to come in a back window, just in case my little shadow was still following me. If he wanted to video tape me being naughty, then he would have to do it from the private property of the neighbor's yard. Surveillance obtained from private property without permission was inadmissible in court. It wasn't much, but at least I wasn't handing the footage to my stalker like I had at Paul's place.

Dropping from the roof, I took my keys from my bag and ran the half mile back to my jeep. I was about to take some personal time.

* * *

As I entered the club, I heard Ben singing and girls

screaming. The combination mixed with the fading adrenaline of snooping through an occupied house and deepened my convictions. Tonight was the night. If I couldn't get a reaction out of Ben with what I was about to do, then I would never get a reaction out of him.

Emily found me and motioned to my outfit as she pantomimed an exaggerated gasp.

"Girl, you look ama-a-azing." She dragged the word out as her eyes looked over me approvingly. Her words gave me confidence. If Emily said I looked good, I looked good.

In the back of my mind, something didn't feel right. It took a moment to pinpoint what it was, and when I did, I smiled. Ben had missed his cue and Aaron was revamping his guitar solo. I slipped a glance to the side to see if there had been a reason for this—hoping there had been a reason for this.

Ben was looking straight at me, mouth open with his hand strumming out of pure reflex. Luckily he wasn't looking at my face; otherwise he would have seen the look in my eye and known what my presence at his concert that night was all about. As it was, I looked back to Emily before he ever knew that I had seen him.

"So where are these guys you told me about?" I yelled over the music.

Emily smiled wickedly and wrapped her arm around me. "Right this way."

True to her word, they were hot, and I was even more annoyed than ever that I wasn't attracted to any of them. They were only tools to me. Why couldn't they be more? What I would pay if any of them could be more.

Introductions were made, glances exchanged, evaluations made, and the game called Single Life was on. I had a choice between two of the six, the way I saw it. I could choose the eight-to-five-I-shop-at-Nordstrom's boy or the I-live-at-the-gym-don't-you-want-to-touch-my-arms man. Choosing the one I thought would intimidate Ben the most, I made eye contact with Muscle Man.

"Hi," I said over the music.

"Hi," he echoed, his eyes involuntarily dipping downward. "Wanna dance?"

Definitely the right choice. "Absolutely."

He put his drink down, took my hand, and led me to the floor. Gritting my teeth, I let him. Ben's band was playing a fast song, and most of the crowd was bouncing to the beat, but none so much as Muscle Man, who hopped and twitched like a fish out of water. I glanced over at Ben, but he seemed to be purposefully averting his eyes.

As Muscle Man brought himself back to earth for a slow song and moved in, I became more discouraged. Ben was singing to a group of girls and appeared completely unconcerned with Muscle Man's advances. My plan to ensnare Ben was failing, and at the same time, I was being turned into a boy toy by a complete stranger. Life was not fair. I wanted to go back to work where I had control over everything.

"You want a drink?" Muscle Man yelled into my ear when I once again dodged his lips at the end of the song. Applause filled the air, and I nodded.

What was I doing?

"Water," I said, and we headed to the bar where he ordered.

"You've got some pretty good moves, girl. What's your name?"

"Rhea," I replied without a smile.

"Ray? As in Raymond?"

"Something like that."

"Oh," he said nodding and sliding my water to me.

"So what's your name?"

"Jaxon."

"Good to meet you, Jaxon."

"Yeah. You too."

We were officially out of things to say.

The next song started, and Emily came up behind me.

"Hey, hottie, wanna dance?" she asked me, and in that moment, she was more welcome to me than a guardian angel. Happy to escape, I took her proffered hand and returned to the dance floor, where Emily and I danced until a man she was eyeing from across the floor came and stole her away. No sooner had she left when two familiar figures moved in to take advantage of my solitary state. Jaxon had my back as Nordstrom boy took the front, "seducing" me with his Gypsy-Man-in-Dockers dance. I smiled, trying to disguise a laugh. He smiled back and moved in.

Closing my eyes in an attempt to block them out, I tried to think of a polite escape. Everything would be so much easier if Ben would just do what he was supposed to do and come rescue me himself. I couldn't make a scene, seeing how this whole night was designed to prove to Ben that I had other options, just like he did. It would be completely counterproductive to allow him to see that I didn't want my other options, even though it was obvious they were interested in me.

A little too interested for my liking.

I was still debating the best course of action when a voice called, "Incoming!" We all looked up just in time to see a group of people hand off a body surfer in our direction. Jaxon and Nordstrom reached up to pass him on. There was a boom and a whack, and then other hands grabbed the surfer as he was passed on.

Nordstrom Boy was holding his eye, and Jaxon was rubbing the back of his head, both in obvious pain. I looked back at the surfer and couldn't help but smile. Ben's eyes murdered me repeatedly and in multiple ways as he floated along on the sea of hands. My heart breathed a sigh of relief. Deliverance never looked so good.

He would certainly have a few words to say to me now.

I turned back to my dance partners. They didn't look too happy as they tested their injuries with their hands and cursed. I was moving toward them when my phone vibrated, giving me a jolt. Fishing it out of its hiding place, I checked the caller ID. It was Kay.

"Hello?" I yelled above the insanity.

"I know you said 11:30, but I just thought I'd let you know that two of your bachelors are rendezvousing."

She had my full attention. "Where?"

"At the factory. They're getting out of their cars as we speak."

"I'm on my way. Thank you!"

"Oh, you will soon enough. Tag, you're it." She hung up. We only "tagged" each other when we knew we were giving the other a career boost. I crossed my fingers and prayed that's what she was doing. My eyes found Emily's, and I pointed to the phone and shrugged my duty to obey it. She understood that to mean I was leaving and frowned, bringing her hands up into an imploring pose. I shook my head and turned to the exit without so much as a backward glance to my dance partners. They had more pressing things to worry about than saying good-bye to me.

Not wanting to draw attention by running, I walked as fast as physically possible to my jeep. It was parked on a side street about two blocks away, but it felt like a mile. I had just turned onto the side street when I felt a shiver move up my back.

There are many different kinds of shivers: cold shivers, eerie shivers, scared shivers, and then there are dark-alley shivers. This wasn't a typical dark-alley shiver, however. It was a fight-or-flight shiver that grew stronger and more paralyzing with every moment. My stomach twisted, my fists clenched, until finally, of their own volition, my feet ran. Unsyncopated footsteps behind me told me that I was not being paranoid. I was being chased. To my right,

I saw my shadow projected onto a brick wall by the surrounding street lights. I looked from my shadow to my assailant's. He was practically on top of me, and I was just about to pass my jeep at full speed. There was no way I had time to get in.

So what next? Whatever I did, I would need to do it fast, because I was just about to be fly-tackled by someone with very heavy footsteps.

Acting on pure instinct, the next time my left foot hit the ground I spun on it, swinging my right foot around in a hook kick I'd always practiced but never thought I'd actually use. The fact that it connected at the base of my pursuer's skull was an act of God. Pressing my weight into my foot, I drove the guy off his feet and head first into the ground. I nearly tumbled down after him as he hit like a fallen tree, head clacking hard against the pavement.

The guy was huge! Or at least compared to me he was. If he got up, it would be like a pit bull facing off against a Jack Russell Terrier. The latter might be more light and nimble, but given enough time, everyone knew who was going to win that fight.

Recovering far too quickly, the guy scrambled, trying to get to his feet. Knowing the moment he was up on two legs I was in deep doo-doo, I fell back onto my training and snapped a kick right into his tailbone, feeling a sick pop that corresponded to his cry of pain. His tailbone was broken but he was still pushing onto his arms, trying to stand.

Who was this guy?

Motions quick, I straddled his back, dropping a strike to the base of his skull to daze him as I bent down and wound my arm through his for a shoulder lock. He felt my leverage too late, trying to roll me, but I widened my stance over him and levered his massive arm until he screamed and I felt his joint strain.

I had him. We both knew it.

"Hi, my name's Rhea. What's yours?"

He muttered something. I couldn't make it out exactly, but

it didn't sound nice. I decided to try again.

"So, do you always chase girls in the dark, or am I special?"

It didn't take a mind reader to see he was furious. That my hook kick had landed was pure luck, and we both knew it. I was just going to have an easier time living with it, was all.

"I think you broke my nose," he sputtered, clearly confused to be in the position he was in. I'm sure he was betting the little chase scene would end differently. Looking at his squat face and cauliflower ears, I didn't feel an ounce of remorse. The guy was a trained fighter who had been set on taking me down. Had he gotten his hands on me, who knows what would have happened.

"Sorry. Accident," I said. A very fortunate one. "Now why have you been following me? Who hired you?"

"None of your business."

"Really? Because I totally thought it was my business."

He cursed and tried to muscle out of my lock, forcing me to push in and crank his arm to an even more awkward angle. His massive biceps made it easy.

"You want to make this hard for yourself? Fine, I'm up to making your life hard right now." Sliding my hand a little higher on him, I jammed my thumb into a bundle of nerves on his neck, causing him to gasp. "Now stop forcing me to hurt you, and just tell me who hired you!"

There was no reply, just a shuddering breath. I had made a grown man cry. It didn't feel as good as I thought it would.

It was hard not to yell. "Why are you following me?"

His voice came out as a growl. "It's my job."

Oh, yeah. The man hated me. "What's your job?"

"Same as yours," he said. "Only I do more than you."

"Obviously," I said with heavy sarcasm. "Who wants me followed and why?" I could guess, but it would be much better if he told me.

"I'm not going to tell you that, lady. Clients don't come

back if you rat them out. Now could you let me up? I'm choking on blood here."

"You're lying on your stomach. All the blood's headed for the pavement. You're fine."

He cursed, trying to twist his way out any way he could. I wasn't going to get anything out of this guy unless I went all Hollywood on him. And even if I duct taped him to a chair and threatened him with tray of sinister dental instruments, he still probably wouldn't talk. That put me in quite a predicament.

I couldn't very well keep him in a shoulder lock all night, but if I let him go, he could just follow me. Calling the cops would lead to statements and filing charges, forcing me to miss my opportunity to find out what was going on at Jock Stock. Decisions, decisions. Every option had a flaw, but I chose the one that might turn out the best. If I left him where he was, someone was bound to find him soon, weren't they?

"For the record, I would really like to just let you go and have us both go our separate ways," I said. "But since we both know you're not about to let that happen, you really give me little choice."

Abruptly leaning forward, I levered his shoulder until I felt it popping out of socket. As expected, the man's head arched back, trying to compensate for the pressure as he cried out in pain. The window of opportunity was small, since the guy was far from an amateur, but I took it, shooting my left hand forward to loop around his neck in a rear-naked choke. I quickly dropped my shoulder lock to let my left arm grip the inside of my right elbow and snuggle in for sleepy time. Squeezing in on the arteries of his neck with all I had, I hung on for dear life as he thrashed for a couple of seconds before growing still.

Knowing he could be playing possum, I quickly counted to two before letting him go and lowered his head to the cement like a sleeping baby.

Man, the guy was heavy when he went limp!

Checking to make sure he was pulse positive, I hesitated before leaving. What if he woke up in a matter of seconds? What was to keep him from following me then, or getting someone else to do so if he had a GPS on my car?

I gave him a quick pat down and found a cell phone and scrolled through his address book. No name was listed under "Keith" but there was a generic "K" number. I could check all the numbers in his phone against Jock Stock employee listings later, plus taking the phone could buy me some time. The pit bull would have to get to another phone before calling whoever he worked for—if he had the number memorized. I grabbed his wallet, swiping his driver's license for good measure. Devon Ferguson. It was good to know one's enemies. Plus, now I knew the address to send his phone back.

I loved it when things worked out tidy.

Devon groaned as I picked his pockets, making me nervous, so I gently gripped his neck and took him under again, making sure his pulse stayed strong as I did so. At this rate, he would wake up long before I made it to Jock Stock and alert whoever was there that I was coming.

A quick glance around showed no one else on the street, but I was running out of time. Eventually I would be spotted if I didn't get moving and some good Samaritan would put my stalker back on the path to taking me down again. I had to do something to slow him down . . . and since I was already emptying his pockets, why not just take his pants altogether? And his car keys. Maybe it would teach him not to chase little girls in the night.

I didn't think. I just acted. The pants came off in a flash, his boot-cut jeans sliding smoothly over his weathered combat boots without a hitch. Checking for a pulse one last time, I left, pants in hand. My entire body shook like I was on an extreme caffeine rush, but I didn't allow myself another glance at the motionless figure. I just got in my jeep and drove off.

NINETEEN

MY LONG-SLEEVED black "work" shirt slid smoothly over my club top and, grabbing my backpack, I jogged the distance to Jock Stock. As promised by Kay, two cars were parked in the parking lot. Paul's and Keith's. Who'da thunk? I didn't see any sign of Kay, though. She had called me just under twenty minutes ago, but twenty minutes was a long time when it came to spying on suspects. The question now was how was I going to spy on them at all? They were in a secure building, which had doors that beeped when you slid your card to open them. Sneaking up on them seemed out of the question.

The patter of rushing feet behind me distracted me from my discouraging thoughts. Expecting another surprise attack, I whipped around to face my assailant.

"Don't kill me!" Kay cried, holding her hands up like a white flag. "What took you so long?"

"I'll tell you later. Can you tell me anything?"

"Nothing! We've been trapped out here waiting for you." We? That meant she brought her cameraman along for this ride. "It looks like you were right, Rhea, but the station doesn't want me to broadcast until I have something solid. When can you get me your info?"

"Tonight or tomorrow," I said and turned back to the

building. I needed to get in there. Fast. "Did you get footage of the cars?"

She rolled her eyes as if to say, *Puh-lease!* "Hurry up and get me the scoop, will you?"

I grunted an agreement, trying to figure a way into Jock Stock without alerting my subjects. Treating a deep breath like a pep talk, I started toward the building.

"What are you going to do?" Kay called after me.

"I don't know yet. I'll make it up as I go along."

"You're crazy! You're my inspiration, but you're crazy. You know that?"

I smiled but didn't turn around to let her see it. Paul and Keith meeting at work on a Tuesday night? How stressed did they have to be to do something so dumb? And how could I get in to see what idiocy had brought them together? My only hope was the delivery entrance in the back. The all-access card Martel had procured for me should get me past electronic security, as long as one of the keys on the key ring in my bag was to the massive steel door in front of me.

Fishing the keys and card out, I started with the most industrial-looking key and caught my breath as it slid right in. Biting my lip in hope, I held the card up to the reader, waiting for the light to blink green before I twisted. The dead bolt unlocked.

Hallelujah!

Creeping into the lower warehouse area, I was careful to shut the door with minimal sound, immediately finding myself in the pitch black of an empty factory that reeked of glue. Restashing the keys and card in my bag, I found my flashlight and placed my hand over the light so only a dim glow lit the room when I flipped it on.

I moved quickly, having no problem finding the security door on the opposite side where the break room and factory entrance were, but if I swiped my card, the sound would echo all around the factory and up the hallway. Or, maybe it wouldn't be so loud. Maybe I was overreacting and should just go for it!

Not seeing another choice, I was about to chance it when I looked up the stairs and saw Paul and Keith had left the corporate office door open on the second floor. There was no way they wouldn't hear the beep in this big cement box. I was stuck.

Cursing, I moved away from the break-room door, looking for another option. The sci-fi bubble hall seemed to be the only way into the offices, but Jason had said Martel built it so he wouldn't have to walk through the factory. So how did everyone get to the offices before? Fire code would require there be a fire exit aside from a glorified catwalk, and I needed to find it.

A door shut above me, and I heard the rumbling of male voices. They were leaving. I had missed the whole thing. Operating completely on instinct, I raced to the break room door again, hand poised and waiting for the beep from the door above me so I could swipe the lower door as an echo. It worked, and I raced to the front window facing the parking lot and whipped out my Super Ear for when they came out. The silly thing could hear through glass, and if those two guys were talking when they exited, I was going to hear it.

I waited a minute. Two. It felt like an hour, but at last the front doors opened. I aimed the receiver at them.

"It's just a case of dumb luck," Paul was saying. "I just didn't know when I came on, but we have to work together from here on out, or this all comes tumbling down."

"Agreed. If one of us points the finger at the other, we'll both go down, and with the PI watching, who knows . . . "

"I know," Paul's voice agreed softly.

"But we can protect each other quietly if we don't change our social dynamics."

One of their cell phones rang, and it was Keith who picked up.

"Hello? . . . Oh, Devon, yes. How's our girl?" My stomach sunk. That would have been me. "What? Where are you? . . . Headed to the hospital? How long ago did you lose her? . . . Well, do you know where she was headed? . . . Fine, send me the bill." He clicked the phone off with a slap. "It looks like our girl's on the loose."

"What happened?"

"I don't know. I guess Devon wasn't as good as he said. It sounds like she beat the crap out of him."

"Why would she do that?"

"He didn't say," Keith replied.

Paul gave a nervous look around. "We should leave. I don't feel safe here."

"Agreed. Any last questions? After this, I don't want to have to risk meeting and talking again before we do it."

Do what?

"No, I've got it."

"Fine, then let's get out of here."

They moved to their individual cars, and I could almost hear Kay's voice in my mind, directing her cameraman on where to shoot and when to zoom. This was her kind of Tuesday night.

Keith's car was the first to pull from the parking lot to the main street, and Paul's car wasn't far behind him. Once they were out of sight, I breathed easy and beeped myself out the employee entrance, making sure it locked behind me. Headed the direction where I had last seen Kay, I waited for her to pop out of the shadows.

"Did you get anything?" she asked the moment we laid eyes on each other.

"Not much. I basically just got their good-byes—"

"Did they set up Martel?"

"Oh, yes," I replied and tried not to laugh when she smiled. "I think they were both embezzling separately and set off flags when they tripped over each other."

Even Kay looked surprised at that, shaking her head. "Two

guys embezzling from the same company? Martel sure can pick 'em."

"No joke. They're teaming up now to catch each other's backs."

"That kind of arrangement sounds like it could easily blow up in their faces. They must have an exit strategy by now. It's not like they can keep things going."

"Paul could," I confessed. "Or he could if I hadn't found his angle. I'll make up the report once I've got Keith figured out. I'm still not sure how he pulled his off, but I think you're right. I think they're both going to pull out now and move on while they're in the clear."

Kay's expression went carefully blank as she considered something.

"What, Kay? Spill."

"No," she said quickly. "I just was thinking."

"About?"

"It's probably nothing, but I want to get out of here. Want to come to my place for a drink?"

I nodded. Why not? "See you there."

It had been too long since I spent a night with Kay, and it would be good to talk th.ngs out with someone who had a conniving brain.

* * *

Kay's dabbling in tabloid writing hadn't quite gotten her the penthouse she wanted, but she still had a sweet view of L.A. from her twenty-eighth-floor apartment. Kay hadn't always been high maintenance, but it came quite naturally to her once she tried it on for size. And she'd never gone back.

Only the best for Kay. And if it wasn't the best, she threw it back. Unfortunately, I think she picked up that last quality from me.

A carton of chocolate soy milk sat between us on the coffee

table that was otherwise covered in Keith's receipts. Looking over them, Kay took a gentle sip from her glass as if testing fine wine. Chocolate soy milk was one of Kay's rare indulgences. The woman counted calories like a human Body Bug.

"It sounds like you almost have everything tied up on this one," Kay said, angling to face me on the couch. She'd pulled her hair back into a casual ponytail before changing out of her designer suit and into designer sweats. The woman didn't beat her body into machine-like stamina like I did, but she hit the treadmills and had the body to prove it.

In truth, her looks were a little too provocative for a career in newscasting. She would never be an anchor unless she waited twenty years and worked some wrinkles into her skin. Until then, she could just keep on using her looks and her insane knack for flirting to be the first on breaking news wherever she went.

"I'm close," I said. "If I could just find a 'Martel' ID with Keith's picture on it, my part in this whole drama would be over."

She swirled her glass around, watching the brown liquid coat the glass before gliding back down. "But where did he funnel the money from? This is a lot of money to miss for any company, regardless of size."

"Definitely. It's like an entire person's salary," I agreed, and we both froze.

"Did you look into that?" she asked, eyes hopeful. "Payroll fraud?"

I hadn't. I had looked into all the employee files and checked their pay stubs, but I hadn't checked to see if an extra paycheck was going out to a non-existent person every two weeks. As CFO, Keith was also in charge of payroll. Creating a fake employee was completely in his jurisdiction.

"Now I just feel stupid," I said, and Kay grinned from ear to ear.

"That's why you keep me around. But how did you know it

was him if you couldn't find money funneling to him?"

"Disneyland," I said. "He paid for a family trip with his credit card but didn't use his personal account to pay off his balance last July."

She smiled, eyes smug. "I love that you found that out before the police and that I get to be the one to tell them. They get angry, and my boss may give me a raise."

I laughed at that, knowing for certain that she would ask for one. She deserved it too. The news station paid her less in a year than I typically made in a month. How was that fair?

"Sometimes I think there isn't anything you can't do," Kay said.

Me? She was the one who had just handed payroll fraud to me! "Uh, I would beg to differ with you on that one."

"Name something!" she demanded. "Name something you cannot do."

"Crochet," I said quickly. She smiled, but shook her head.

"No, you choose not to crochet. You could if you wanted to. I wish I could be as good a reporter as you are a PI."

"Stop that!" I said quickly. "You're a fantastic reporter, Kay, and if you don't feel that way it's only because the station limits you and holds you with such tight reins. Left to your own devices, you would redefine the news."

She lowered her eyes modestly, not having a response to my praise. She wanted me to be right, and I knew I was. Arguing would have been futile. Instead Kay laughed. "Look at us. Here we are on a Tuesday night with nothing better to do than talk about work. Aren't you dating anyone?"

"No, but neither are you."

"I know, and we're both good-looking, successful girls with money. What's wrong with men? Why don't they want us?"

"Clearly because we're pathetic," I said, grateful to be with the one person in the world who didn't pester me about Ben. In fact, ever since our senior year of college, Kay had advocated against me dating Ben, but never mentioned why. It still gnawed at me.

That said, we both knew why I was single. Why Kay was single was a baffling mystery in and of itself.

"To being pathetic," she said, raising her glass between us.

"Pitifully so," I said as we chimed glasses.

"Now, you have a story to tell me," she said, nestling in and getting comfortable. "One of us was at a club earlier tonight dressed in full-on hoochie gear. Spill!"

And I did.

TWENTY

IT WAS past one when I made it home, and was still a half a block away when I saw Ben's pick-up in my driveway. With Ben's actions fresh in my mind from telling Kay, I felt excitement race through my exhausted body. If he'd been waiting for me all night, then he was mad. If he was mad, that meant he cared, and if he admitted that, then things might change. I was ready for change.

I pulled into the garage, and Ben appeared in the driveway when I stepped out of my jeep. He hadn't changed from the concert, and his sleeveless shirt only served to enhance his avenging angel pose.

"Where have you been?" he asked roughly, and my heart kicked against my chest, already fantasizing how this would unfold.

"Out," I replied vaguely, starting for the entrance of the house knowing—hoping—he would stop me.

"Oh, no you don't," I heard him mutter, and two steps later he whipped me around to face him, his hands painfully gripping my arms. If life were like the movies, he would have kissed me then, passionately and with confidence, knowing deep down I wanted it. But this wasn't the movies, and he didn't kiss me. He held me at arm's length and glared at me.

"What did you think you were doing tonight?"

Stay calm. Keep it casual. "I was just having a little fun. No big deal."

"No big deal?" he echoed. "Rhea, you came half-naked into a room full of drunk men, and allowed them to do whatever they wanted to you!"

"So?" I heard myself retort, and both of us were surprised. I pressed on, unsure what else would leave my mouth. "Those are the kind of girls you like! Haven't you always said so? I'm twenty-four years old, and I'm single. The good girl act obviously isn't getting me anywhere fast, so I thought I'd switch tactics."

Ben's look of shock mirrored my own internal shock at what I had just said. "Rhea, you are not one of those girls!" His eyes were full of wrath, and I felt a strange pride that I had put it there. "Sure those girls always have boyfriends, but have you ever noticed their turnover rates? They go through them like rental videos, upgrading, repeat renting, and sometimes getting one they know is dumb just to fill the time. Then they accidentally get pregnant and boom! A one-night stand just became a lifetime sentence. You're better than that, Rhea!"

I stared at him. Dancing at a club had just turned into single motherhood. My mind didn't dare process the thought. Instead it thought of things to say to antagonize him further.

"Ben, we both know that's not going to happen, I just wanted—"

He shook me ever so slightly. "It always starts out small, Rhea, but you put yourself in bad positions often enough, and pretty soon bad stuff starts to happen. Just trust me, okay? Stay good. Like your mom said, you want a man who will love you and respect you for who you are, not someone who will use you and then leave when they discover you have a personality."

Ouch. He didn't think a guy would think my personality was worth sticking around for?

Okay, Ben. This is the part where you tell me you are that man who loves the real me, and then you soften that vice grip you have on my arms and kiss me possessively and passionately!

I'd seen it happen in so many movies that I half expected it, but apparently Ben and I hadn't been watching the same movies, because he was totally off script.

Well, if he wasn't going to follow the script, neither was I.

"Is that how you are with girls, Ben? What's your longest been? Three weeks?"

"That's different."

"Different because you're a man?" I said, shocking myself with my own bitterness. "I'm sorry, but there's no double standard here. What goes for one goes for all."

"Besides," he said, thinking of something—someone else. "I'm careful."

"And you think I wouldn't be?" The shouted words echoed between us in the garage. It took me a moment to understand why I had yelled them because I certainly didn't mean any of it. I realized I was arguing with Ben simply to prove that hypocrites can't preach. I argued with him because that was all we seemed to do anymore—even the silence between us lately was nothing more than fight avoidance. He was chastising me because, for one night, I had acted like the kind of girl he was attracted to. Even when I stooped down to his level, he still didn't seem to get that I didn't want to play "sister" anymore.

Call it misdirected hormones. Call it what you will, but in that moment I was an inch away from kissing him out of sheer frustration. But I didn't. I just stared him down, and he stared back. His eyes dropped to my work shirt.

"Well, I'm glad to see you at least put some clothes back on," he grumbled, reaching out to adjust the neckline.

"Not really," I replied, tempting fate. "I'm wearing the same thing underneath. I just put this on—"

"I don't need to know," he interrupted and backed away.

"You just really surprised me tonight, Rhea. I never thought I'd see you act like that."

Guilt. He was playing the shame card on me, which was definitely unfair, hitting way below the belt. I couldn't let him see that it affected me, though.

"I guess there are a lot of things you don't know about me." My voice sounded cold, almost indifferent. I applauded myself.

When our eyes met again, his were panicked and mine were cold. He looked truly worried, and I knew I wouldn't hold up against his tender eyes very long. His mouth opened as if to speak but then shut with a snap.

"Fine. It's your life." He walked off, muttering something else under his breath I was sure I didn't want to hear, and I panicked. He had come all the way here because he loved me. Not the way I wanted him to, but as the brother I never had. I couldn't let him leave feeling as if that love was unappreciated.

"Ben!" I called and waited until he stopped and looked at me before continuing. "Thanks for saving me tonight. I really appreciated it."

A smile broke through his previously stern features. "Yeah, well, I may not do it again if you're going to make a lifestyle out of it."

"I don't think you have anything to worry about," I admitted, and his smile broadened. For the first time in months there was a comfortable silence between us.

Then he left.

I watched his truck pull away as the garage door shut between us, feeling strangely at peace with what had just transpired, even though Ben hadn't followed my script. I guess that's what actual movies are for. With the flip of a switch, I could live vicariously through the actors on the screen. It was definitely a night for a hopelessly romantic flick.

TWENTY-ONE

I WOULD HATE to be a police officer. One of the great things about being a PI is that I can know who's guilty and act on it without having to prove it. Police officers not only have to prove guilt; they have to obtain their information in such a way that it is admissible in court. Ninety percent of the information I have acquired on this case is inadmissible because, well, I broke the law to get it. I don't make a regular practice of that. It just happened to work out that way this time. One good thing is that I most likely will not be used as a witness, and if I do my job right, the prosecution won't need me.

My report made it clear: Paul defrauded the company with a dummy website. I was hoping that later, when I filled in the blanks, I would be able to say that Keith did it through payroll fraud. The numbers in Paul's column added up all nice and pretty, painting a damning picture for him. He was going down, but I needed Keith for the charges against Martel to be dropped. It was kind of sad that Keith's Disneyland adventure had been the big mistake that led to his downfall. Something just seemed wrong about that, but I wasn't going to think about it too hard.

I glanced at my watch. It was 7:15 in the morning. I grabbed my protein shake and took a sip, debating the wisest course of action. Should I call him? Should I just show up at his office? Was his office bugged? Did any of that matter now that I'd sent

Keith's guard dog to the hospital? Had he been a lone wolf, or was someone covering for him?

These were questions I didn't have answers to as I reached out for my phone and dialed Martel's number. He answered on the third ring.

"Mr. Martel? I was wondering if there is any way we could meet on your way to the office this morning."

"Why?" Martel sounded stressed. "Do you know something?"

"Where would be a good place to meet?"

"My office would be good."

"No, it would not be good. Any other suggestions?"

"I, uh . . . sometimes I get bagels for everyone. I could stop by today. Do you know where Earnestine's Bakery is?"

"I can find it. What time?"

"Twenty minutes," he said after a moment's deliberation.

"Great," I agreed. "See you there."

I hung up, went straight for my keys, and pulled up Google on my phone. I would get there a little early and watch for any familiar or lingering faces just in case door-to-door perfume salesmen didn't work alone.

* * *

Martel was right on time, and when he didn't see me, he got into line anyway. Good for him for acting normal! I hung back and watched to see if anyone would take notice of him. To my annoyance, no one did, but if they had half the equipment I did, they could be listening to us from across the street. I had to assume the worst.

I took a pen from my backpack and grabbed one of Earnestine's napkins.

Your phones are tapped, Candace's too, maybe more. Sorry to report that you have two embezzlers in your office: Paul and Keith. Don't say anything out loud, I don't know if we can be heard. Full report coming soon.

Taking my place behind him in line, I pretended to look over the menu until Martel noticed me, and when he started to speak, I shook my head. He took the hint, and we waited our turn.

It wasn't until after he ordered that I casually brought my hand to the counter and slid the note in front of him. He reached to pick it up, but I once again shook my head. If he angled it right, then someone could read it from across the street, but I didn't say this aloud. He looked at me like I was insane, then read the note from the counter. From the corner of my eye, I watched as his eyes widened and his jaw set. When he looked away, I crumpled the napkin into my hand and placed it in my pocket.

"Have you ever had any of the smoothies here?" I asked him. He looked baffled for a moment.

"I've never tried them myself, but I hear they're good," he replied.

"My friend Amanda says they're real good," I added, and he flashed me an incredulous look. I winked at him and smiled.

"Is that so?" was all he could say. "Tell you what, you pick one, and I'll put it on my tab. How does that sound?"

"Great! That's real nice of you, mister."

We continued our corny conversation until at long last money was exchanged for purchases and we were out the front door.

"Keep me updated," he said as I walked him to his car.

"Yeah, you too." We shook hands, and I returned to my car with my free smoothie. This guy was really starting to grow on me.

* * *

Candace's wary eyes met mine as I walked in the front

door of Jock Stock with my list of the eighty-seven employees currently on payroll. If I was lucky, this would be the last time I walked in this building at all.

"Hi, Candace," I greeted, and she nodded in return. "Can I speak with the warehouse manager?"

"Mario?" she asked, confused as to where I was heading with this course of investigation.

"Yes," I said, looking over my list. "What's his last name?"

"Gomez," she said, picking up her phone and dialing his extension. I found his name on my list and highlighted it with my green marker. One more down, and not counting my previously accounted-for suspects, that meant seventy-eight left to go.

"Yeah, Mario?" Candace said into the phone. "Can you come to the main lobby? Someone would like to speak with you . . . Yes, now . . . Thank you." She hung up. "He'll be right out."

"Thank you," I said, and we fell into an awkward silence. The kind of silence that was full of questions.

"So, who do you think did it?" I asked, just to get the ball rolling.

Her eyes snapped up. "What do you mean?"

"I mean, who do you think framed your boyfriend? You've got to have a guess, and this is your last time to go on the record before I turn in the report."

Her eyes met mine before looking around to make sure we were alone. "Well, there's no way Delores did it, and I know Amanda didn't either, and Jason may have used you, but that's no reason to try and pin it on him!"

"Used me?" I echoed, confused.

"Yeah," she said, her voice wavering a little and her eyes scrutinizing. "He told us about it. That night after the party . . ."

When she didn't continue, I prompted her. "What about that night after the party?"

"Well, afterward, you two . . ." She must have seen the look on my face because she changed the ending of her sentence. "Didn't you?"

"Are you saying that Jason told everyone we slept together?" I was trying not to laugh.

"Well, yeah." Candace seemed less and less sure of herself.

I laughed out loud then, the way only a frigid virgin can when accused of promiscuity. "No," I said finally. "And if you want eyewitness accounts, I can provide them for you, although I did see him getting it on with someone the night after our date. Maybe he got me confused with the other girl."

"You were spying on him?" Her indignation was laced with wonder.

"Only until I realized what I was spying on," I said, hoping she wouldn't push for more.

She smiled a wicked grin before it faded, her mind moving somewhere new. "You really didn't sleep with Jason?"

"I swear it," I said, crossing my heart with my finger. "We kissed, but that was it."

She bit her lip, eyes dropping. "We're kind of friends. He's always talking about all the women he's been with, and I never know how much I can believe him."

I decided to keep things upbeat. "In his defense, he is pretty smooth, but let's just say that due to circumstances beyond his control, I am not available to him."

Candace nodded her understanding. I don't know exactly what it was that she understood from what I said, but I could tell that she believed me.

"I just want to call him on it one of these days, you know? Make him shut up."

It occurred to me then that Candace was attracted to Jason. Tempted by him even as she loved Martel. I wondered how many women felt that way and what life must be for the little boy with a Jaguar.

"You've got the better man," I said as I pushed away from her desk and looked at my watch. "Stephan wants a relationship. Jason doesn't know what he wants." And that's all I was going to say about that. Any more, and Candace and I would start meeting for lunch and sharing manicure appointments. No thanks.

What was taking Mario so long? Candace was eyeing me like she wanted to ask me some other intimate question when a worker came in behind me and headed to the factory break room.

"Hi, Florence," Candace said, and the woman waved back as she swiped herself in to the factory area.

Maybe I didn't need Mario.

Handing Candace my clipboard with the highlighter, I pointed to the names. "Will you do me a favor and mark any of the names of employees you have personally met? Only people like Florence, where you can connect a face with a name."

"Sure," she said, popping the lid off and marking the page without hesitation, her hand moving swiftly down the rows, skipping few names. When she handed it back, only six names were not green.

"Thank you," I said, glad to see some candidates still on the map.

"Sure. What's that for?"

Behind me, Mario pushed into the room. "What is it, Candace?" he asked. "We're slammed."

Candace pointed to me.

"Hi, Mario," I said, holding out my hand for him to shake. He gave my hand a firm pump. "Quick request," I said, handing him the clipboard. "Would you highlight any of the names of workers you know that are still blank?"

His eyebrows furrowed as if not understanding my question before shooting a cautionary look to Candace. She nodded.

"Fine," he said, taking the clipboard from me. He glanced

over the remaining names, swiped the marker four times, and handed it back to me. Two names remained. An east coast sales rep, and a man named Aaron Woodside, who was listed as a warehouse employee."

"You've never met him?" I asked Mario, pointing to Aaron's name.

His jaw clenched. "Nope."

I glanced at the paper just to make sure I had the job description right. "It says Aaron Woodside has worked in the warehouse for two and a half years."

"Not in mine, he hasn't," Mario said with confidence.

I hid my elation behind a grin. "Thank you, Mario. That's all I needed."

He glanced at Candace. "I can go?"

"Yes. Thank you, Mario," she said, and he was gone.

I turned to meet Candace's thoughtful look. "Hard worker," I said, bringing the list her way again to show the last name on the list, the east coast sales rep. "Ever talked to this guy?"

She shook her head. "He's an independent contractor. Doesn't take our stuff too seriously from what I can tell. Makes a few sales a year. Nothing special."

I nodded. It would be easy enough to see if the guy was real once I got back to my office. I was betting, however, that Aaron Woodside was my winning horse.

*　*　*

Many means and methods are readily available to those bent on being involved in criminal behavior, but some methods are more popular than others. What most perpetrators of fraud do is weed through death certificates, which are public record, and find someone their same sex and about their age who has never been issued a social security number. Such individuals are usually children who died at young ages and whose parents never thought to go through the process of getting them a social security number. Criminals, however, are more than happy to have a social security number issued and a card sent to their home. As soon as they have that, they usually work to obtain credit cards and go on spending sprees. By the time the credit card companies catch on, the scammers are long gone and pulling the same stunt with someone else's identity. That's why I was not surprised to discover that Jock Stock's Aaron Woodside had never bought a car or owned a home in the Los Angeles area. It was also why I wasn't surprised to find that his only known street address belonged to a Jamba Juice. And that's why I knew I'd find the name Aaron Woodside on the death certificate of a child who had died in 1973 of SIDS with no social security number on it.

At long last, I had something solid on Keith.

The man hadn't used the deceased child to get some credit cards. He'd given the kid a job. And since Keith was the one who managed payroll and signed all the checks, he could easily direct deposit the check without anyone being the wiser. Martel thought he had one more employee than he actually did, and Mario never saw the books that showed he was one pair of hands shy.

So simple.

Again, the case connecting Aaron Woodside to Keith was circumstantial, but it was compelling enough to get the ball moving in the right direction. Luckily for me, though, I showed accounts for Aaron Woodside at Bank of America, and they had security cameras. Even if Keith did everything online, a warrant from the police could tie all the activity to personal computers, and he was still screwed.

Now if I could just answer the million-dollar question: If Keith was doubling as Aaron Woodside, why in the world was he "tripling" as a second Stephan Martel?

I didn't like it. Not even a little. I'd been hired to find one embezzler, and I'd found two, and I still hadn't solved the original problem. That was going to eat at me.

Unless, of course, Martel had been embezzling from himself all this time. Wouldn't that just beat all? Most companies were limping along just trying to survive, while Jock Stock was gushing with financial leaks and still staying in the black. Martel should write a book.

Whatever the case may be, I needed to make up my report on Paul and Keith and get it to everyone who mattered. I may not yet have a perfect grip on how Keith's wormy brain worked, but I had enough to put at least two men in handcuffs, and if I waited on that, they might run. If they got away because I held off on a report, that was on me. Plus, there was reasonable cause to believe that Keith was behind the account in Martel's name, which was something the police and IRS could handle much better than I could, now that I was handing them the "who," "what," and "how."

Elliott would contend that I was done. I'd been hired by Martel to prove that Paul was embezzling. Lucky for me, he was. Handing Keith's activities in the same report was a pure bonus, and if Martel wanted me to connect Keith with the secondary accounts in Martel's name, he would need to hire me again. We had the footage of Martel repeating over and over that I should ignore everything else and just prove that Paul was stealing from him.

Mission: accomplished. I was technically done, albeit unsatisfied.

Changing back into my "mowing" clothes, I went into my home office and updated my report on Keith, and then printed all I had on Jock Stock's two embezzlers, making four folders. Only the police could do what was needed to be done to refocus the case. One copy of the report would go to them, one to Elliott, another to Martel, and the last to Kay—as promised. I'd show the police all the evidence I had found so they could try to obtain it legally. They'd pull a warrant out of their hats with amazing speed, considering the questions pounding them from the media (aka Kay), and Martel could breathe easier and have someone to point at regarding the accusations against him.

I felt unusually tired as I grabbed my files and headed for the door. I shouldn't be. I had hit my one-week mark for a full payday. I should have been mentally high-fiving myself on a job well done. I'd solved a case without resorting to using my ninja bracelet even once. Ben would be so proud.

Ah, Ben again. Why did everything always loop back to him? And was it a coincidence that I wasn't looking to create closure with my case any more than I was working for closure with Ben? Was I starting a trend of leaving things half finished?

Did it even matter?

Gathering my newly printed files, I headed out to my jeep.

*. *. *.

I walked into the police precinct half an hour later, feeling guilty and trapped the moment I stepped inside the door. I don't know why precincts make me feel that way. Maybe because I know how many laws I've broken and how many times I could have been led in there on an involuntary basis.

Officers milled about around me, and I was careful not to get in the way of their obvious urgency to get from point A to point B. People have asked me why I never joined the police force. I needed only to look at my surroundings to know exactly why such a career track had never been a temptation for me. Everyone around me wore the same uptight uniform with the same pained expression and even seemed to have the same personality. Everything here was serious, at least to my civilian eye. Maybe that was another reason I felt trapped. It was ninety-two degrees outside, and these guys were all in stuffy, hot, dark uniforms while I wore a tank top and shorts. I'd take my job any day.

The officer at the front desk ignored me until I cleared my throat to catch her attention. Only then did she focus her haunted eyes on mine and ask an otherwise pleasant question.

"How may I help you?"

I shivered despite myself. "I need to speak with the lead investigator on the Stephan Martel case for Jock Stock."

"And your reason for speaking with him?"

Translation: *And I want to save the dolphins. Your point?*

"I am a private investigator, and I have evidence to submit to him regarding the case."

She looked to her computer screen, finding it more important than me. "Well, he's not in right now and may not be for the rest of the day. Would you like to leave it with me?"

"No," I said, mirroring her tone. "I would like to give them to him myself. Is there anyway he can be contacted and told that I have important evidence pertaining to his case?"

"He is not available for appointments until Friday. Would you like to make an appointment for then?"

Not with you, I wanted to reply, but I didn't. "Sure. I'm available anytime he is."

She looked over his schedule. "How about 8:30 in the morning?"

"Fine. My name is Rhea Jensen."

She wrote it down, not caring that she spelled it wrong. "Have a good weekend, ma'am."

I was dismissed.

"Same to you," I replied and left fuming. Why didn't anyone take me seriously? Okay, maybe I shouldn't have worn shorts, but that was beside the point! Truth was, the same attribute that worked so well for me in my job also worked against me when it came down to it. Oh, well, I would give Elliott and Martel their copies of my file, give Kay her head start, and consider myself finished for a long weekend. No more work. I was free. Free to do what, I didn't know. I couldn't remember the last time I had a weekend off. I would have to stick close to Emily.

Making my way to my jeep, I called Kay.

"Bad time," she said when she answered.

"No worries," I replied. "I just wanted to let you know that I'm turning my report into Elliott, but the secretary at the police department is making me wait until Friday to meet with the detective on the case."

"You're finished?"

"Yup. All done with my part. Still have some loose ends, but I'll let the police take it from here. But like I said, they won't see me till Friday."

She let out a throaty laugh. "Poor baby. Were they mean to you again?"

"Maybe," I pouted.

"Their bad. So I assume Martel's in the clear since you're giving me the file."

"Ninety-nine percent chance," I said, hoping it wasn't a lie.

"Beautiful. When can we meet?"

"I thought this was a bad time."

"It just became a good time," she said, and I heard a door shut on the other end of the phone. "Where are you?"

I glared at the ugly brick and glass building in front of me. "At the police station."

"I'm, like, five minutes away. Stay where you are, and I'll be right there."

"Fine. I'll see you in a few, then."

We hung up, and I gazed at the police station uneasily. I should have told her the coffee shop on the corner. It wasn't too late, but five minutes was five minutes, and there was free parking at the station. I could stick it out like a brave little girl, and I did—breathing easier when Kay's hybrid pulled up and she hopped in the passenger seat of my jeep.

Glancing over my outfit, she gave short laugh.

"Don't say it," I sulked.

"I don't have to," she said, taking the file. "You do it to yourself. The Hiltons could shop in your closet, and you go out on official business dressed like that?" She rolled her eyes and started reading. "Admit it, you like it when cops treat you bad. You'd feel too guilty if they were nice and end up confessing all your sins in a fit of guilt."

I shot her a look, wondering when she got so insightful.

"As far as I'm concerned, you can wear tassels the next time you come." Her voice was distracted now as she absorbed the contents of my report. "This is great stuff, Rhea."

"I know. Poor Martel. He was getting it from both sides."

She shook her head in disbelief. "Paul was taking credit for all Internet referrals, while Keith was stashing the money under someone else's name? How did you learn all this so fast?"

"I ignored ethics," I said, checking my rearview mirror out of habit.

"Well, it'll be a great story," she said, shutting the folder. "Do Keith and Paul know you know this?"

"They shouldn't, but then again, I shouldn't know what I know either."

Kay's face turned thoughtful.

"What is it?" I asked. "You got that same look on your face the other night. What are you thinking?"

"Just be careful, Rhea. I've got a weird feeling."

"About?"

"About these two guys. What brought them together? What are they planning?"

"I don't know, but my work is done. They're not my concern anymore."

"But you are still theirs," she said, tapping her teeth together in a rare show of worry. "Be careful for as long as they're still free, okay?"

"Of course," I said. "I'm always careful."

She did not look consoled.

"You really are worried, aren't you?" I teased.

"Fine. Laugh about it. Maybe I am wrong, but I have good instincts, Rhea. I know you do too, but just be doubly careful, okay?"

I gave a small salute. "Aye-aye, ma'am."

She rolled her eyes and turned back to her car.

"Have fun!" I said, realizing that I couldn't wait until Friday to leave the file for police. I would have to leave it with the mean secretary.

"You know I will," she called before hopping into her car and driving away.

Getting back out of the jeep, I walked back into the precinct and tossed the report on the front desk, the female officer scowling in annoyance. I didn't give her a chance to speak. "Tell the lead detective the media has all this info and they'll be contacting him. Let me know if he wants to move up his appointment." I pushed away from her desk, not letting her speak, and walked out, head high.

Man, that felt good. And the fact that more than one Officer Friendly checked me out as I swaggered out the door didn't hurt either. Life was better when I didn't let it walk on me.

Now if I could only pull the same attitude in my personal life.

TWENTY-TWO

MY CASE done, the invoice filed, and my ninja bracelet getting a new addition in the shop, I found myself with nothing to do. You'd think that with everything that was going on, I would have been all riled up, anticipating the resolution of my case. Instead, I was pulling a business card out of a Book of Mormon and making the most unlikely of phone calls.

I hadn't read any more since Saturday, but THE OOK OF RMON continued to stare at me. It was one of the infinite things in my life I left unfinished, like Ben. And if I wanted to work my way up to resolving things with him, I had to start with the small things that didn't mean as much to me. The book in my hand weighed on my conscience for reasons I didn't understand, and I knew it wouldn't leave me alone until I let the missionaries tell me their little message. I'd meet with the elders, let them do their little dance, and then I'd have one less item of unfinished business in my wake.

What could it hurt, after all? I'd give them thirty minutes of my now-available time, and then I'd move on to something else on my list. Maybe something ambitious, like telling Camille she needed to have her private romantic dinners at her fiancé's place. I'd have to tell Emily to pop some popcorn for those fireworks.

As the missionaries' phone rang, I was expecting—and nearly hoping—to get voice mail, but Elder Wright's voice answered. Crap. I was really doing this?

"Hey, Elder, do you remember a girl you ran into on the street a couple of days ago and gave one of your books to?" I could almost see the young man stop in his tracks.

"Yes, I do. Is that who I'm speaking with?"

"Yeah, are you busy right now? Because I have some time open, and for some strange reason I am in the mood to let you guys preach to me."

It was obvious that he was stunned. Well, so was I.

"Sure! Where are you now?"

"Not far from the place we met. Where are you guys?"

"Wherever you need us to be," was his endearing reply.

"You choose the place," I said, suddenly regretting my impulsive phone call. What in the world was I thinking?

"How about the Getty Museum in twenty minutes?"

"Sure, sounds good," I said nervously and hung up before I changed my mind. Five seconds later, my phone rang, and I smiled, secretly hoping it was the missionaries calling back to cancel. If so, I would take it as a sign that their message wasn't for me.

No such luck, though. It was Kay.

"Hey, girl!" she said when I picked up.

"Hello yourself. Didn't I just see you?"

"Yeah. Where are you headed?" she asked, but her voice had a pinched quality that made her sound nervous.

"To the Getty. How about you?"

"Just finished up for the day. Do you want to do something tonight?"

It is difficult to describe how odd of a question this was coming from Kay. Kay is a red personality to the core and derives all her pleasure from successfully completing difficult tasks. Never, in all the time I have known her, has she asked if

I wanted to do "something"—as in something unspecific. Add that odd question to her pinched voice, and I felt as if I was talking to an imposter.

"Something, hmm?" I teased. "Kay, is everything okay?"

She groaned. "Rhea, you know me better than is healthy."

"So what's up then?"

"Nothing, really. It's just . . . I just . . . "

"Just what?" I prompted when she couldn't finish the sentence.

"I've just got a weird feeling, okay? So my night's clear for anything you want to fill it with."

Strangely flattered, I gave a little laugh. "Sure. I've got a few things to do, but then, yeah, let's do something."

"Okay." She sounded relieved. "I'll look around and see what events are available, okay?"

"I leave it in your hands."

As we said our good-byes and hung up, I smiled. Some people find Kay difficult to deal with, but all in all, she's a great friend.

* * *

Outside and sitting across from each other in a private nook, I looked over my instructors of the Mormon faith. Elder Gonzales was tall and lanky, and his somber expression seemed to be ever present. Elder Wright, on the other hand, seemed to be bursting with excitement to be meeting with me and unable to wipe the smile from his face. I looked at him the most, because his energy was contagious. It was a good thing he was at least three inches shorter than me; otherwise I might have been attracted to him.

"So, you guys aren't really named Elder, are you," I accused.

The ever-somber Gonzales gave me a practiced reply. "No, Elder is a title we take upon ourselves as missionaries."

"Oh," I said, even though I didn't understand why in the world such a measure needed to be taken.

"So, did you get a chance to read the book we gave you?" Elder Wright asked, unable to contain himself.

"Not all of it," I replied. "I only got to Jacob."

"Really?" he asked in surprise.

"Yeah, and I know I'm not finished with the book, but I was wondering if I could ask some questions anyway."

"Absolutely," Wright said, smiling again.

"Okay," I began. "So I get that this book is supposedly about the ancient American Indians and that it says these people believed in Christ and had prophets like the Jews—well, I guess they were Jews, weren't they? Jews that were cast out of Jerusalem for preaching Christ." I was trying to keep it all straight in my head, but it was a lot to remember. "Whatever. Basically, they believed in God, they believed in Christ, they believed in revelation through prophets, and they wrote everything down. My question is, who are these people supposed to be in our modern history? Mayans? Zapotech? The infamous Aztec? All of them?"

The two boys stared at me, and I was beginning to worry until Elder Gonzales opened his mouth.

"Most people believe in a supreme being, even if they call it by different names," he said. I furrowed my eyebrows, wondering if he understood my question as Elder Wright shook his head at his companion. Elder Gonzales fell silent.

"We don't claim to know who they are," Elder Wright said simply.

I was surprised by his answer. "But how do you expect people to take this seriously if you don't have any evidence to back it up?"

He didn't even blink before he replied. "There is a way to know that this book is true that goes beyond adding up the evidence."

"Oh, really?" I asked skeptically, and he nodded.

"Pray. Ask God. He knows who you are and will tell you in your heart and in your mind that it is true. Did you read Moroni's promise at the end of the book?"

"Didn't make it that far," I said. "Only to Jacob, remember?"

"Of course. Well, would you be willing to read that promise with us now?"

I shrugged. "Sure."

"It's found in Moroni 10:3–5," he said as he opened the book and handed it to me. "Will you read it out loud?"

Casting a nervous glance around to make sure we were still alone, I decided to play along. "Sure," I agreed and then saw that the verse had already been highlighted for easy identification. I took a deep breath. "Behold, I would exhort you that when ye shall read these things, if it be wisdom in God that ye should read them, that ye would remember how merciful the Lord hath been unto the children of men, from the creation of Adam even down until the time that ye shall receive these things, and ponder it in your hearts.

"And when ye shall receive these things, I would exhort you that ye would ask God, the Eternal Father, in the name of Christ, if these things are not true; and if ye shall ask with a sincere heart, with real intent, having faith in Christ, he will manifest the truth of it unto you by the power of the Holy Ghost.

"And by the power of the Holy Ghost ye may know the truth of all things."

Birds chirped in the silence as I handed the book back to Elder Wright.

"What do you think about that verse?" Elder Wright asked, making the mistake of asking me what I thought about the verse as opposed to what I felt about the verse, which was fine. I wasn't ready to tell them how I felt anyway.

I shrugged. "It's a nice thought, if nothing else."

"I know that it's true," he said intently. "If you pray about the Book of Mormon, then God will tell you in your heart, through the power of the Holy Ghost, the truth."

"Okay," I drawled, unnerved by his intensity. "Fine. I'll do that, but on my own time. I've got twenty-five more minutes before I have to get back to business. What do you guys have to teach me that I don't already know?"

The elders shared an unsettled look, and I knew my demeanor was making them uneasy, especially Elder Gonzales. I can be a tough audience when I choose to be.

"Well, God created a plan so that each of his children could return back to him," Elder Wright started in a rehearsed voice and I was impatient just listening to him.

"Yeah, I got that part. It's your sister's favorite verse, remember? We all have the choice to choose good or bad and receive our rewards accordingly, with Christ set up to make up the difference. I like how that prophet Nefee describes it—"

"Nephi," Elder Wright corrected. "We pronounce the 'i' just like the letter's name."

Good to know. "Okay. I get what I read in here, but your sister said that I should listen to you and pray about what you taught me. So what do you have to teach?"

Elder Wright's mouth opened and shut once before words actually filled them. "What religion are you?"

"None," I replied honestly. "I personally don't believe any religion is God's favorite religion. They're all just messed up politics." The elders looked as if I'd struck them, so I quickly added, "No offense intended, of course."

"None taken," Elder Wright said smiling again. He took out a paper. "You know, I haven't yet learned your name."

"Rhea," I said quickly, feeling slightly embarrassed. "I guess I kind of just skipped introductions, didn't I?"

"No problem," he said and then looked me straight in the

eye. It was the same look he had given me the week before, and it made my heart feel like it was being tickled. He cleared his throat.

"Rhea, before you came to this earth, you lived with our Father in Heaven." He paused, and I got the chills. "You were very much like who you are now, only you did not have a physical body." He handed a paper off to Elder Gonzales, who started drawing a picture.

For the next fifteen minutes I didn't make a sound. I just listened to Elder Wright and Elder Gonzales as they took turns explaining God's plan to me. Even though my heart was pounding in my chest, and I felt as if I were glowing, I tried to look at the plan they were presenting to me as clinically as possible, and just when I thought I had found its fatal flaw, they brought up baptisms for the dead. As twisted as the concept seemed to my brain, it made sense and filled the gap for all those who lived without access to teenagers in name tags.

Everyone, dead or alive, would have the opportunity to fully accept God and Christ before they had to face them in judgment. The way I saw it, the plan was slightly biased toward people who were already dead, but then again, what did I know about the afterlife?

"How do you feel about what we have just taught you?" Elder Gonzales asked.

I shrugged, unwilling to show them my true reaction. "It makes about as much sense as anything else I've heard. It beats damning unbaptized babies and everyone east of England. If nothing else, you Mormons cover the bases. I'll give you that."

Elder Wright was watching me carefully. "May I ask you a personal question?"

Personal questions . . . I didn't do so well with those. "Maybe."

"Have you ever been baptized?"

Oh. He thought that was personal? No problem. "Sure. I've got godparents and everything. My parents may not have been churchgoers, but they didn't skip over that detail when raising me."

"And the person who baptized you, with what authority did he baptize you?"

"I'm sure he had a degree," I replied with disinterest.

"Let me rephrase that," Elder Wright said. "How did the priest who baptized you get the authority from God to do so?"

I blinked twice, surprised I hadn't considered the question. "I'm sure he didn't. It's just a symbol, after all, of our willingness to obey."

He nodded. "You're right about the symbolism, but it also must be done through the authority of God."

"Why?" I asked and by the look on his face, I don't think anyone had asked him that before.

"Because God is a god of order," Elder Gonzales volunteered. "He does not allow just anyone to run around and do things in his name. That would be chaotic."

Good point, and instinctively I agreed, but then thought of all the religions of the world and how they fought against each other. "So what about Catholics and Protestants and Muslims and stuff? Why does God allow them to behave as they do?"

"Keep in mind," Elder Wright said, "that God is not at the head of any of those religions. Men are."

I noticed a man watching us and wondered if he had heard what was just said. "I wouldn't say that too loud around here. It's not very PC."

"I did not come on my mission to be politically correct, Rhea. I came to teach the gospel of Jesus Christ in its fulness. Joseph Smith saw God and His Son, Jesus Christ, and reorganized His church for the last time on this earth. It will never be taken away until all the will of God has been brought to pass and every person has been given an opportunity to join its ranks."

I wanted to laugh, and I would have, were it not for a burning I felt in my heart. I didn't speak for a moment as I reassessed my new acquaintances. They looked normal. Elder Gonzales looked like the type of guy who would become a scientist or engineer and sport the same haircut and glasses for the rest of his life. Elder Wright looked like a trainer in a gym and the type of guy who would string girls along. On a scale of 1 to 10, he was at least an 8 as far as looks were concerned, and yet, instead of strutting around on Muscle Beach, he was going door to door trying to teach what he considered to be the plan of salvation. And as much I wanted to laugh and walk away from these two young men, something held me to them—to Elder Wright particularly. His eyes somehow captivated me, and every time I looked at him, I felt as if I should know him better than I did.

"Rhea," he said softly. "Will you pray about this and ask God if this is His plan?"

"But not before we finish the discussion," Elder Gonzales said a little tersely.

I was surprised and intrigued by the tension that built between my two teachers. I definitely wanted to hear the rest. "Oh? There's more?"

Elder Wright looked reluctant. "Yes, but we could probably save it for another time."

I looked at my watch. "I've got about ten minutes. You can use it however you want."

Elder Gonzales didn't hesitate for a moment. He launched into the Mormon health code, which he referred to as the Word of Wisdom. I sat back and listened to his rehearsed presentation and limited myself to checking my watch only once. When he was done, a slightly flushed Elder Wright began lecturing me on the importance of chastity, clarifying that sex was an act that should only take place between a man and a woman who were legally married.

"So no homosexual relations?" I asked, thinking of the first time I had met them.

"No," he said, looking slightly anxious. Luckily for him, I was straight, and Kay wasn't sitting next to me. If she had been, we'd be in for an evening of Proposition 8 debate. I bit my lip and debated bringing it up, and then I saw Elder Wright tense as he sensed the direction of my thoughts. He'd probably had the conversation a thousand times. Rehashing it was useless. And besides, I had to get going.

"Rhea," Elder Gonzales said, taking control of the conversation. "We promise you that as you live these laws that God has given, he will bless you in your life."

"I'm sure He will," I replied. Elder Gonzales looked at his companion as if he were supposed to say something, but when Wright wavered, he spoke in his place.

"Rhea, we would like you to commit to these laws that we have laid out for you, and we promise that as you live them, the Spirit of the Lord will bear witness to you that they are good and true."

I checked my watch. Time was up. "No problem," I said. "Anything else?"

They looked at me as if I had just turned into a fruit bat.

"All of it," Elder Wright reasserted. "The coffee, the alcohol, smoking, sex . . . everything."

"Understood," I said. "I'm out of time. Anything else you want to make me promise?"

"Yes," Elder Wright said quickly. "Will you be baptized?"

Now it was their turn to change into fruit bats.

"Excuse me?" I said in open shock. "You want me to become a Mormon?"

"Yes," he said with so much energy that it felt like an electric wind slammed into me.

That was probably the one question I was not ready for. Silly me. What else did I expect from missionaries? What surprised me more was an insane little voice inside of me that was telling me to agree to his offer. The experience was becoming entirely too surreal for my liking.

In an effort to avoid their gazes, I looked down to the drawing they had made for me. It was hardly art, but it walked me through the lesson they had just taught me. It was then that I saw its genius. I smiled and gave a quick laugh, which was undoubtedly not the reaction they were looking for.

"What?" Wright asked.

I pointed to the first of the three circles. "I get it. According to your plan here, if I accept your offer, get baptized, and lead an exceptional life, I've got a chance of going to this really exceptional place, right?" I pointed to the top circle, which Elder Gonzales had labeled "the Celestial Kingdom." "But if I refuse your offer to get baptized while I'm alive, then the best shot I've got is to get into this place you call 'the Terrestrial Kingdom,' which is basically like getting eternal second place, and that's only if I accept a proxy baptism someone does for me after I die." I pointed to the bottom circle. "And if I don't get baptized here or accept a proxy baptism, then I go down to this 'Telestial' place. Talk about a catch-22. You guys are sneaky."

Elder Wright stared at me a moment, mouth hanging open. "I have taught that principle I don't know how many times, and no one has ever gotten it like you have."

I shrugged, standing from my bench. "I get paid to see things clearly."

"You must be good at your job," Elder Wright said, standing as well. "You didn't answer my question. Will you be baptized?"

I smiled and didn't allow the flock of butterflies in my heart to sway me. "I honestly don't think that's a decision I can make with the amount of information that I have, Andy." He flinched at my use of his first name. Maybe he didn't know his sister had written it in her testimonial at the beginning of the book. "But I'll read more and let you know what I think. Is that good enough?"

"And you'll pray?" he pressed. His eagerness was so adorable, probably because I couldn't recall a time in my life when a cute guy had begged me to pray.

"Yes, I'll pray."

"Can we have your number to follow up with you? We noticed it was blocked when you called earlier. "

I faltered, but then shook my head. "Not for now, okay? I'll call you."

"Okay, then."

"Thanks for your lesson!" I smiled at Elder Gonzales, who stuck his hand out toward me. I shook it and then turned to Elder Wright to do the same.

"Would it be okay if we ended with a prayer?" Elder Gonzales asked. Yet another question I wasn't ready for. I looked around at all the bystanders and shook my head.

"Maybe not today, okay?"

He didn't like my answer but nodded anyway. "Okay. Next time."

"Okay," I agreed, trying not to be amused by his complete case of tunnel vision. "Well, thanks for the lesson, Elders."

"Anytime," Elder Wright said eagerly. "And there's more where that came from if you want to give us a call."

"I'll remember that," I replied and turned away. It felt so weird to walk away from them. I felt like I was doing something wrong, but I didn't slow my pace or look back. I had other things to worry about before I started considering the validity of "The Plan" they had laid out for me. I would have plenty of time to think about all that after the case was officially closed.

At least, that's what I thought.

TWENTY-THREE

YOU NEVER plan to be abducted, especially when you are a black belt in three different forms of martial arts and have just come from talking to people who want to baptize you into their church. The thought that two men might casually walk up behind you, bash your head with a metal pipe, and then cover your face with a chloroformed towel isn't really on your top-ten list of concerns.

But that's what happened to me when I left the elders. The next thing I remember was being bounced awake. My head felt like a cracked egg, and the first sensation that greeted me was extreme pain starting at the base of my skull and rushing down my spine. The second was sightlessness—total and complete darkness. The third was motion. I was in something that was moving. I rolled onto my back in hopes that my head would move less if it were on something solid. I almost cried when the floor jumped beneath me. I was going to die. Right there, in whatever coffin I was in. A rolling coffin.

A trunk. I was in a trunk. I realized this as my hand reached out and touched metal and carpet simultaneously. That would also account for my sensation of suffocation. I took a deep breath, reached to my side, and found . . . my cell phone? They hadn't taken my cell phone? What kind of kidnappers were they?

I unhooked it from my belt and lit up the screen. It said it was 3:09 p.m. How time could fly when you were having fun! Unable to think well enough to dial, I pressed my first speed dial button. It wasn't until after Kay answered that I realized the level of my incoherence that I called her instead of the police.

"Rhea? Is that you? Thank God! I thought you were dead!"

How did she know I was in trouble? "Almost," I muttered. "They've got me in a—"

"A car. I know, I know! I'm right behind you, girl. I've been with you all the way. I knew this was going to happen. I don't know how, but I did. I should have warned you better. Look, they're taking you toward Malibu Beach." Her voice was shaking, and even in my dazed state I knew she was hysterical. She took a deep breath and let it out slowly, purposefully calming her breath. "It's good to hear your voice. I thought I had lost you!"

"Need to call the police," was all I could say in response.

"They're on their way. I have them on the other line. Rhea? Don't fade on me, Rhea!"

"Going to—" Instead of saying "throw up," I actually did so, and Kay endured it.

"Rhea, turn your head to the side. We can't have you breathing that in. Rhea? Can you hear me?"

"Yeah," I said and began gagging.

"Rhea, turn your head to the side! Do you understand? Do not talk to me again until your head is turned. I mean it, Rhea! After all you've been through, you do not want to leave this world by asphyxiating on your own vomit!"

She had a point, and although it nearly killed me, I managed to turn my head. Then I groaned.

"Good, you sound better now. I'm right behind you, Rhea. Don't you worry, you're going to get out of this, okay?"

"Cops," I said.

"I told you, they're on their way."

"Gotta call them."

"I did—" She sounded exasperated when I hung up on her. I dialed nine-one-one.

"Nine-one-one emergency. What is the location of your emergency?"

"I'm in a trunk," I managed.

I heard the tap of the operator's keyboard. "And where is the trunk located, ma'am?"

"A car."

The operator started to say something else, but I didn't hear. I was choking on my own bile.

"Ma'am? Are you okay?"

I didn't have enough energy to answer stupid questions. "Kathryn McCoy," I said instead.

She hesitated. "The newscaster?"

"Yes," I rasped.

"Kathryn McCoy has you in a trunk, ma'am?" Her voice sounded honestly shocked.

"No, she knows where I am."

"I see," she said before pausing. When I heard the tape played back to me later, it seemed impossible that she had only been silent for two seconds, because in that time I had nearly blacked out. I jumped awake when I heard the operator's voice again.

"Rhea?" How did she know my name? "Ms. McCoy is on the phone with another operator right now and she is leading us to your location. We're only minutes behind you. Ms. McCoy would like to relay the message to conserve your energy and she'll take care of you. Do you know the name of your assailant, ma'am?"

"Keith Barlow. Paul Bradley. They framed Martel. Stole his money."

"Who is Martel, ma'am?"

I felt the car slowing, after which it turned sharply. There was a low rumble, like a garage door, and the car came to a stop. Without another word to the operator, I clicked off my cell phone and reached around for a place to hide it. They couldn't find out that I had talked to someone. That would make them panic, and I needed them to be calm. I felt a toolbox and tucked my phone behind it before rolling back into the position I first recalled waking up in, all the while trying to avoid my vomit.

Car doors shut and a male voice spoke authoritatively. I listened carefully but could only make out the words "over there," "bring," and "ask." There was the sound of shoes on cement as the owner of that voice circled to the trunk. When a key was placed in the lock, I swear I felt my pulse in my throat, but stayed motionless as the trunk was lifted, and fresh air and light surrounded me.

The unfamiliar male cursed, and I knew exactly why. I was lying in the reason.

"You're paying for me to get that cleaned up," he said to one of the other men.

"No problem." It was Keith. I hadn't heard him before. The other man spoke again.

"I'll raise her up so you can put the bag on her head."

Moments later, a hand cradled the back of my neck and pulled me into a sitting position. For a second time I was surrounded by darkness as a canvas bag slipped over the top of my head. Then I heard metal and my heart sank as my wrists were handcuffed behind my back.

Of course I'd be handcuffed only days after I talked myself into waiting to outfit my Swiss Army bracelet with the tool to get out of them. Instead, I left the makeshift tools that might have saved my life in the cup holder of my jeep. Smooth. But this was an embezzling case, for crying out loud! Who got abducted and handcuffed in an embezzling case?

"Wake-up time, Rhea," the car owner said, after which my nostrils were filled with the most indescribably foul smell imaginable. I gagged, coughed, and lurched all at the same time, teetering on the edge of throwing up again. The tough guy sensed this.

"Whoa, keep it down, little girl. Otherwise you'll be swimming in it. The bag's not coming off for anything."

I kept it down. Barely.

"Now we're going to help you walk a little ways. Do you think you can stand?"

I nodded a reply, but it was unnecessary. They had already pulled me from the trunk to my feet and were leading me . . . somewhere. Being in no position to do anything else, I followed until they spun me around roughly and one of them raised my arms back behind me.

"Feed the pole between her arms," the tough man said, and I realized there was a third man with us. If Keith was holding me on my right and Tough Guy on my left, that meant someone else was sliding the metal bar between my arms. I wondered how many other people were silently watching on.

"Bend over," the man commanded, and when I didn't immediately respond, a punch to my stomach persuaded me. I didn't realize what was happening until I felt them back me up and something metal graze along my back and nick my head. I was then pulled backward, and I stumbled into a sitting position onto what felt like rubber tire, with my back leaning against a piece of rounded metal. After a moment of deliberation and a little use of imagination, I decided that I had been successfully attached to a tetherball pole.

"Stand up!" the car owner commanded, and knowing I would receive "help" should I not comply, I did so. "She's all yours now."

It was silent with the exception of dress shoes on cement

and the sound of my labored breathing within the fabric surrounding my head. The footsteps came closer.

"Hello, Rhea. I think you know who I am, right?"

I nodded. All of a sudden I was dealing with the Godfather.

"You've been quite the little problem child for me. You know that? Now, I brought you here because I need you to answer a couple of questions for me. Can you do that?"

All I could think was that Kay was right behind us, the police were on their way, and that this guy was the most amateur criminal I had ever dealt with. It was like he had learned to be a criminal by watching prime time TV. I nodded my head again, hoping to get him monologuing until the cavalry arrived.

"You know, I never imagined it would come to this. I have a sister your age, only she's happy just dating, buying clothes, and looking pretty. What are you out to prove?"

My cue to talk. How would a screenwriter reply? "Nothing. I just try to help people solve mysteries."

"Is that right?" he mused. "Then maybe you can help me solve a few mysteries."

"If I can," I agreed. "But I charge by the hour."

The stiff backhand that clocked me didn't come as a surprise, even though I'd been hoping all Three Stooges would let my snarkiness slide. Under the canvas I smiled, knowing I could buy time by riling them up.

"Oh, I have a feeling that shouldn't be a problem for you," Keith said, voice smug. "Let's start easy. Number one, what tipped you off that I was the one you were looking for?"

Ah, the most predictable of questions. "Well, I suspected you when I discovered that there was no corresponding withdrawal to account for you paying off your Disneyland vacation."

Any time, Kay . . . She had said she was right behind me and that the cops were right behind her. Weren't they supposed to be reading Miranda Rights by now?

"How about me?" It was Paul's voice. Or at least I assumed it was. It reflected the same curiosity and nerves that Keith's had.

"You both did a great job, but it didn't take too much research. I mean, if I could find out in a week, the police are bound to catch on sometime, don't you think?"

"Yeah, we'll see about that." It was Keith again. "They don't seem very eager to exonerate Martel, do they?"

Blah, blah, blah. I wanted to record these guys and play them back to themselves so they could hear how naïve they sounded. "Yeah, but his lawyer only needs reasonable doubt, and he's got two of those with you two."

Once I said that, the casual tone disappeared from Keith's voice, and he must have moved forward because all of a sudden I could feel his body heat.

"How much does Martel know?"

Time to make him nervous . . . if he wasn't already. "Everything I know."

"That's impossible!" he hissed.

"Keep your head, Keith," Paul said. "Don't give her any info. We've already handed her enough. Make her tell us what she's supposedly told Martel, and then we'll decide if we have problems or not."

I wasn't ready when Keith gripped my shoulders and shook me, my head clanking back against a metal bar and making white stars flash across my blackened vision. My head felt light, and I wanted nothing more than to lay down and go to sleep. Just for a little while. Until the pain went away.

"What did you tell him? How did you say we did it?"

There was no reason to lie, and I didn't have the energy for it. "Well, you created a false identity from a baby that died of SIDS in 1973. You got a social security card in Aaron Woodside's name, but instead of committing credit fraud with it, like most people do, you gave him a job and opened a savings account where you deposited his bi-monthly checks." I heard him curse.

"And Paul, you created a bogus website and stole referral credits. Pretty smooth."

Paul swore, hitting something wooden.

"How did you find all this out? Where was the trail?" Keith pressed.

"Oh, trails are easy enough to find in the digital age." I must have sounded sarcastic because my answer earned me another blow to the stomach. I tried to bend over, but the pole wouldn't let me, and it took several seconds before I caught my breath.

"We're screwed," Paul mumbled over and over.

"Just one more question, and then I'm going to hand you over to my new friend here. He wants to know what you did to my old friend that caused him to resign."

"Who?" I gasped.

"The guy you sent to the hospital. What happened?"

I couldn't help it. I laughed, an ugly sound, given the condition I was in. I laughed until tears came, which was about two seconds.

"Shut up! What happened?" he yelled over me.

"So, he quit, huh? What was he supposed to do to me last night?"

"He was supposed to keep you under close watch and make sure you didn't get anywhere near us."

"That's all?" I challenged.

"Answer the question!"

"I did what any girl might do when a guy she doesn't know corners her in an alley." There was still amusement in my voice, and I could tell it was not working in my favor. I was handcuffed to a pole and surrounded by three criminals, two of which I had exposed and ruined. Retaliation on their part was not entirely out of the question. The question was what kind of retaliation were they willing to resort to?

And where were the police?

Paul was ready to run. "Keith, let's get out of here. We know what we need to know. Let your man do his job, and we'll run while we still can!"

"But my wife . . . my kids!" Keith muttered. It was obvious that being discovered had never been part of his plan.

"It's your own fault you got greedy, Keith," I said, not liking the direction Paul was pushing things. This was not a movie, and letting Mr. No-Name do "his job" didn't sound like it ended very well for me. It sounded like it ended with me dead. "Trying to frame your boss was your downfall. If you had just kept funneling the money, you could have died a millionaire. Instead, Paul—"

"Shut up!" Keith hollered at me, and I heard a sound. A non-human sound. A familiar and scary sound. It was the sound of a bullet being cocked into the chamber of a gun. I froze, and in that moment, my throat turned to Velcro. Gone was all my confidence and all my snippy remarks. I was going to die, and all I could think was, *I hope Ben realizes what he missed out on!* The second was completely unexpected. *Will the Mormons really remember to baptize me after I'm dead?*

Where had *that* come from?

"Wait, Keith," I said, my voice calm. "You're clearly new to this business, so let me give you some advice. Introducing guns at this point is very bad for you." He still held the gun to my head even as waves of fear pulsed off of him. "So far, you've . . . what? Taken money that doesn't belong to you? So you'll get a few years in a top-notch federal prison for white-collar crooks. Big whoop! But if you shoot me?" I let my words sink in. "Think about it, Keith. You want your kids to grow up afraid everyone will find out their dad's a killer? You could get life for something like this. Don't be an idiot."

He faltered. I couldn't see it, but I felt it.

"This isn't a movie, Keith," I added. "You pull that trigger and I go bye-bye in a messy spray that needs to be cleaned up. And if you do that, you'd better pray the cops find you first, because I don't even know what might happen if my people find you before they do."

My people. Did that sound ominous enough? True, they were just my friends, but I could see Ben now. Not just him, but all my boys and also Kay devising a revenge from hell. And as nice as it was to know that I had friends who would avenge me, it wasn't something I wanted to put in their court. If there was only one thing I'd learned throughout my career, it was that revenge was the root source of nearly every case that landed in my lap. Revenge was soul-killing, and I didn't want it to be my legacy.

"No one will know," Paul urged Keith softly.

"Oh yeah, that." I had one more card to play. "Another pointer: when you abduct someone, take their cell phone away. Police and news crews are already en route. I called while I was in the trunk and gave them both your names. They know it's you."

The acidic tang of fear-filled sweat washed through the air, and I prayed they knew their only reasonable choice at this point was to run. If they chose anything else, things wouldn't end well for me. I just hoped shooting me was off the table, because my dad would never forgive himself for letting me work in this field. And where in the world was Kay? If she was arguing with her cameraman over the best camera angle, I was going to kill her!

The air around me was still filled with indecision, and for the first time in recent memory, Elder Wright's advice sounded like a great idea!

Please, God, I prayed silently, *don't let me go out this way. I will have so many regrets. I swear, if you let me live through this, I'll stop breaking the law. I'll be good! Heck, I'll even let the Mormons baptize me! Whatever you want!*

Complete peace washed over me, causing me to blink back shock. There was absolutely nothing peaceful about my current situation. My life was in the usual state of chaos it was always in. I always rode my cases into the danger zone. I was known for it—hired for it. And when I chatted up God about leaving the insanity behind and trying life as a good little Mormon, I felt peace?

Really, God? Are you serious? The Mormons?

I felt as calm as a meadow at dawn, and I knew what I had to do, laughing to myself as I imagined what that meant for me. If I lived through all this, I certainly was going to get an earful from a few people.

Fine, then. If I live through this, I swear to you I'll get baptized and be a good little Mormon. Just give me a chance!

It was upon thinking this that I heard the most unexpected words.

"Mr. Barlow? This is Kathryn McCoy with WLAX Los Angeles, and our viewers would like to know exactly what you plan on doing with that gun. Your comments?"

I didn't need eyes to see that my captors were stunned into inactivity, and I could have cried in gratitude. If Kay had come charging in without thinking, they would have taken her down, exacerbating the whole situation. Instead, she turned on a camera and saved both our skins.

"This is live, Mr. Barlow," she said in her manicured voice. "If you could please give us a response."

Silence. My heart pounded five times before Kay started talking again.

"For those of you just joining us, this is Kathryn McCoy, broadcasting live from Malibu Beach, where two employees of Jock Stock, the company owned by Mr. Stephan Martel, have abducted the private investigator who uncovered their schemes and now apparently plan to kill her in cold blood with the aid of a hired assassin." She said it in her somber voice, the one she typically reserved for blazing fires and tragedies on holidays. Apparently I was serious news.

"The question is, will they do it on live TV?" She left a dramatic pause. "Mr. Barlow, if your wife is watching, how do you think she feels right now?"

He didn't get a chance to answer.

"Police! You're surrounded!" a deep voice yelled over a megaphone. "Guns on the ground, hands in the air! This doesn't need to get ugly." Then off megaphone, but still more than audible. "And someone get that reporter out of here! Now! Now!"

I don't who the "now's" were referring to, but I think everyone obeyed. As for me, I simply slid down the pole and sat on the tire, hoping anyone with a gun would forget I existed.

The same officer spoke again. "Do not be smart, Richards! I will shoot you!" I assumed he was talking to Tough Guy. If so, he had a history with the police. Good. That meant Richards was more likely to shoot at them than at me.

"Get down on the ground! Hands behind your head! Do like your two buddies, Richards. Don't tempt us!"

Richards must have tempted them, because shots rang out and it was in vain that I tried to cover my ears. There were a total of maybe five shots in two seconds and then the squeak of rubber soles running on cement.

"Get the paramedics in here!" Footsteps shuffled all around me, and I heard the sound of handcuffs being used on someone else and those beautiful Miranda Rights being recited. Feet hustled and officers called out to each other, securing the location with surprising efficiency. I'd never really been a fan of the cops, but in that moment I was ready to buy a team jersey.

Just as I was beginning to wonder if I had been forgotten, the bag was yanked from my head, and I saw Kay's welcome face right before she threw her arms around me in a hug and didn't even try to avoid the vomit that was smeared all the way down my right side. Her voice quavered as she spoke, her words tripping over each other.

"You're okay! I thought I was going to lose you for a minute there! The cops were still pulling up when that guy pulled out his gun, and I knew they would be too late. I'm sorry, Rhea! It was the only thing I could think to do!"

"Ow," was all I could say as her eager embrace caused the handcuffs to pinch into my wrists.

"What's wrong? Oh! You're still handcuffed." She turned and tried to catch the attention of one of the nearby officers. "Excuse me, but could someone get these handcuffs off this hostage?"

A young officer that looked fresh out of high school trotted over to us, pulling out his keys. He spoke to Kay first.

"Ma'am, we're going to have to ask you to leave the area. This is a crime scene, so if you and your cameraman would allow yourselves to be escorted off the premises, we'll take care of the young lady here, okay?"

"You're going to be okay, I promise," Kay said, pressing her forehead to mine. I didn't have the heart to tell her it hurt.

"Kay, do me a favor?"

"Anything!"

"Keep my name off the news. I don't want my dad to worry. Tell the story, just skip my name."

"No problem," she promised as two officers urged her to her feet. "I'll meet you at the hospital, okay?"

I nodded and gave a sigh of relief when the young officer freed the first of my hands.

"Oh, and Kay?" I called out.

"Yeah?" she replied, forcing her two officers to stop for a moment.

"Tag. You're it."

She smiled then, and so did I. I breathed easy for the first time in hours.

TWENTY-FOUR

THE REST of the night was a blur. I was taken to the hospital to be treated for a concussion and kept overnight for observation. The cops, for the most part, were content to get minimal statements from me and allowed me to rest with the exception of the detective assigned to Martel's case. He seemed intent on asking me the same question over and over again in a thousand different ways. I told him his secretary had scheduled an 8:30 appointment on Friday for me and that I would be glad to see him then.

He didn't like my sarcasm.

Nor did he like it when Kay arrived and showed him the door as only a human-sized Barbie in four-inch stilettos can.

Like I said, some people can't stand Kay, but she's a great person to have on your team in a crunch.

* * *

By noon, the hospital let me go with instructions to take a week off work, if possible. That wasn't a bad idea, and Elliott had the grace to grant it to me. He also informed me that my check was in the mail and that Mr. Martel had called to express his absolute satisfaction with how quickly we had resolved the situation. Charges against him had not yet been dropped, but we were all confident they would be.

After sending my Aunt Sarah home, begging some time for myself, I went to the beach and listened to the waves crash as the sun moved from high noon to the horizon.

I thought of my mom. I thought of life and why I was even on this planet in the first place. I thought of how everything I touched somehow escalated to a boiling point. Suddenly, it wasn't enough to just be a good private investigator and an independent woman. My soul was throbbing with an intensity that made me wonder if the despair would ever go away. If I had died the day before, it would have made no difference to the world. I was a nobody. My life had no meaning. I ran around exposing other people's misdeeds all day, every day. And if I didn't do it, someone else would. I was replaceable. I was nothing.

I could taste the salt of the tears from my face as I wondered why I was alive. Why was it so important for me to live? Could there really be some master plan, or did it really not matter who lived on this earth and what we did while we were here? In the end, was it all just a wash? Were humans just like every other species and one day, like the dinosaurs, all that would be left of us was our bones?

Without ever saying it out loud, that's how I had been living my life: as if what I did didn't matter in the end. That my means justified the end of whatever case I was working on. I'd hurt a lot of people that way, always seeking the thrill in other people's pain. No other PIs I knew ended up handcuffed with guns held to their head, but I'd faced worse. And I'd faced worse because I pushed people until they snapped and justified it all with the knowledge that I had a happy client. Today's client just happened to be Martel.

As I pondered the changes I needed to make in my life, the warmest feeling came over me. I felt as if my mother were sitting next to me, putting her arm around me, and for once making me feel like I was right where I needed to be. I always ran from one thing to another, afraid of what would happen if I stopped. Stopping meant I would have to admit how much I missed my mother. Stopping meant dealing with every heartbreak and every offense I always tried to pretend didn't really matter. Stopping meant facing how alone and useless I felt in the universe.

Yet, there was this whisper of a feeling that told me I was important, and that it was watching me very closely. And that feeling meant something.

Watching the sun sink on the horizon, I spoke to my mom as I would have had she physically been sitting next to me. I talked about everything: Ben, life, finances, my roommates, my job, my hopes, my dreams, the things I was unhappy about in my life, how much I missed her. Everything. When the conversation turned to God, I brought up the elders.

"So what do you think, Mom? You want to be a Mormon? They will baptize you even though you're dead. You always told me that churches were made by men for men, but no one could have just written that book they hand out. What do you think?"

I think I was actually expecting an answer, but all I got was a shiver, and I realized the sun was completely down and the evening chill had set in. I finished things up with my mom and took my time going back to my car, reviewing all the regrets I would have had if I had died the day before. The biggest one was Ben. I had to let him know how I felt.

Back at my car, my cell showed seventeen missed calls, all originating from four people. I listened to each of the messages—laughing at Kay's death threats if I didn't call her back immediately—and saved them all in a fit of sentimentality. The shock of still being alive paired with the fundamental knowledge I had to change or die young had me in a daze that felt suspiciously like peace until the moment I pulled onto my street and saw Ben's truck in my driveway.

He was waiting for me. Of course he was. And knowing that, all the confusion came back. My stomach twisting into a knot, I pressed on my brakes and pulled to the curb as tears formed in my eyes.

I cannot articulate how badly I had wanted him to be with me in the hospital the night before. But instead of reaching out to him, I had gone out of my way to make sure he wasn't informed of what had happened. The truth was that I had come to depend on Ben in ways that he could not provide, and it was killing me. And now I was crying in my car a half a block away from my house just at the sight of his truck. How pathetic was that?

I had to gain control of myself before I walked in the door and saw him. Or worse. Before I walked in the door and threw myself in his arms and begged him not to let me go. Having a gun aimed at your head makes you catalog regrets pretty quickly. My number one regret had been that I had never really allowed Ben to love me the way he might have if I had dared to let him. I had been seventeen and scared out of my mind at the time when we had our shot. In my mind, Ben had been so perfect and such a flirt that I couldn't believe he could be happy with me for the rest of his life. So many other girls wanted him, and I feared that one day he would resent how I had confined him into a relationship so early in life.

So I had civilly broken up with him.

I told him I thought we should both check out other options to make sure we were really what the other wanted. He had agreed without argument and was with someone new the next day.

Sitting in my car seven years later, that still stung, but I pretended it hadn't and played the best buddy role to date. I don't even think he noticed that I had never dated anyone seriously since. Breaking up with him had been a test to see if he wanted me bad enough to fight for me. He hadn't, and seven years later I was still waiting around for him to change his mind.

What would Ben do if he knew that I had been in love with him this entire time? Would it scare him? Did he already know? Had he just kept me around to be nice or because he felt responsible for me? He frequently said how he felt like he had to watch over me—mostly while we were talking about my job.

I leaned my head against the steering wheel and tried to calm down. What was wrong with me? Two minutes earlier I had felt so serene. Then again, serenity is easy when you're in denial. And the truth was, when my father had held my hand at the hospital, I had wished he was Ben. When I had checked my messages, I had wished every call had been from Ben. And just then, turning the corner, I had hoped Ben would be there waiting for me.

And, at last, he was. Why that made me cry, I'm not sure. I think part of being a woman is accepting that occasionally you have no control of your emotions no matter how much you wish you did.

I took a deep breath and checked my mascara in the mirror. With just a little help it looked okay. Lucky for me, I'm not a messy crier. Putting my car in gear, I made my way down the street, pulling up next to Ben's truck instead of into the garage. I didn't want another garage scene. I needed to face him where others were watching us so as to ensure good behavior on my part. My heart leapt into my throat as I ascended my front steps, and I tried to swallow it back where it belonged. It didn't budge.

The first sight I saw when I opened the door was a glimpse of Emily and Ben pulling away from each other on the couch. It wasn't a guilty retraction, more like they had been discussing something private, probably me.

"Hi," I said, shutting the door behind me. "Am I interrupting a party?"

Ben stood and I could tell from the look on his face that he knew about the night before. He rushed toward me, reaching out. "Are you okay?"

I panicked and motioned him away. "Yeah, I'm good."

"Why didn't you call or anything? I would have come to the hospital!" He looked hurt, and he had a right to be. If he had done the same thing to me, I would have been furious.

"I know. I'm sorry. I was just out of it last night, and today I wanted to be alone. I didn't call anyone, I swear. If I had, you would have been the first."

"If you don't mind," Emily interjected. "I think I'll leave."

Both Ben and I nodded and then looked back to each other. Emily walked up the stairs, down the hall, and into her room, and still neither of us spoke. The expression on Ben's face told me that he had something to say, and I waited for him to say it.

"I saw the tape," he said as if it pained him. "Kay showed it to me. They were going to kill you."

"There was that possibility," I said softly.

"Are you okay?" he asked, taking a step closer, and I felt tears sting my eyes again.

"Can we not talk about it?" I tried to say this casually, but a catch in my voice gave me away. I looked away so he wouldn't see the tears fighting their way to the front of my eyes.

"Oh, Rhea," he whispered, and then I felt his arms close around me. Instinct told me to run, but seven years of regret pushed me in. "If those men weren't in jail I would kill them for what they did to you! They better get long jail sentences without parole."

I could feel his breath on my neck, and it sent a shock down my spine. *Tell him!* my mind screamed. I wrapped my arms around him and held him back, ignoring the sharp stabbing pain from my bruised ribs. This. This was what I needed. I had to tell him. It was long past time.

"Rhea?"

"Mm-hmm?" I answered.

"Uh, I don't know how to tell you this. The timing sucks, but the longer I wait the harder it will be, so I might as well get it out now before I lose the nerve."

The tension in his voice set me back on edge, and I pulled my head back and looked at him. "What is it?"

His mouth opened as if he were going to speak, couldn't find the right words. His expression was both torn and resolved at the same time.

"I guess I just have to say it," he said finally, his eyes dropping briefly to my lips. My heart jumped. Was this it? "The guys and I have been booked to open for a national tour. It's a really great gig and," his eyes searched mine again, "we leave tomorrow."

I stepped back as if he had struck me.

He was leaving me? Tomorrow? Right when I needed him most, he was going on the road?

"You're leaving?" I said helplessly.

"If I could put it off, I would, but you know how these things work. If we let the promoter down our first time around, he may not call us for another. Will you be okay with us gone?"

"Of course I will," I said, pushing away from him and heading for the stairs. He grabbed my arm.

"Don't pretend to be tough now, Rhea. You have every right to be shaken up and every right to be unhappy that four of your friends are leaving you."

I stared at him. Unhappy that four friends were leaving me? Was he stupid? Was he blind? I pulled my arm from his grasp and almost made it to stairs before his soft voice stopped me.

"Rhea, please don't leave like this. I may not see you for a while, and I don't want this to be how we say good-bye. I want to spend my last night here with you. I can't pretend I don't want you anymore."

And there it was. I froze mid-step, my defenses completely shattered. Hadn't this been what I regretted most? I had given my heart to Ben years ago, and after years of feeling hollow without him, he was finally taking that step forward. He was finally admitting that he felt the same way I did.

And what did a marriage license and quickly spoken "I do's" have to with that? What did a promise to my mom twelve years ago mean when it interfered with everything I wanted? Sure, I had promised my mother that I would wait for the man who would marry me, but in my mind, that man had always been Ben. I turned to face him. Knowing he had me, he rushed in, whispering my name before his lips crashed onto mine. I whimpered as he held me to him, commanding my ribs to stop complaining for the next little bit and unwilling to tell Ben that my body wasn't quite up for being touched. He was leaving tomorrow. Tonight was the night.

It had been a long time since I had kissed Ben, not since our fateful breakup, and the timidity of those days was long gone. We were two adults who knew what we wanted. He raised me off the ground and easily carried me to my bedroom, kicking the door shut behind us and removing his shirt at the same moment. As we fell back onto my bed, my heart thudded in anticipation while my brain did the most unexpected thing. It pulled up an image of Elder Wright's blush as he asked me to live the law of chastity, with a promise that God would bless me if did.

Where had *that* come from?

From this point on I won't tell you what we were doing, only the thoughts I was trying to ignore as I participated.

I saw myself standing at the throne of God trying to rationalize my actions.

But God! I was protesting. *I had been in love with him for so long and it was my only chance! I know you said sex was only to be had between married people, but I wanted to marry him. Doesn't that count for anything?*

I didn't hear God's response, but I got the feeling that he wasn't impressed with my case. No doubt millions of others had sung him my very same song.

It would take months for me to discover that the next words to go through my mind were a paraphrase of some verses I had only read once while sitting in front of Paul's house. At the time, I hadn't even taken notice of the words, but they came loud and clear as I argued with God in my head.

> For the atonement satisfieth the demands of his justice upon all those who have not the law given to them. . . . But wo unto him that has the law given, yea, that has all the commandments of God and that transgresseth them. . . . O the vainness, and the foolishness of men! When they are learned they think they are wise, and they hearken not unto the counsel of God, for they set it aside, supposing they know of themselves.

The words hit me with such force that I froze involuntarily for the barest of moments. Ben didn't seem to notice. I had the law, I knew this was wrong, and I was doing this anyway. No matter how I looked at it, it was a sin.

Then another thought struck me. If the Mormons were right, and only they had authority to baptize me, then that meant any sins I did before then didn't count! Didn't they believe baptism washed you clean?

Aha! A loophole! I pled that case before God, and although in this scenario He agreed that I had wisely played the system, He did not approve. In my mind I felt guilty before Him and told Him I had regretted my decision my entire life.

I considered that. Would I really regret doing this for the rest of my life? I had waited so long for Ben to notice me again. How could I ever regret the consummation of my love for him? It didn't seem possible, even though the mental image of my anguish before God seemed so real. All I knew was that I needed to decide real fast before all my mental debates became moot points. Ben was not taking things slow.

In fact, if I took myself out of the moment, I would have to confess things weren't going how I imaged they would at all. His motions were mindless, demanding. The actions of someone who knew they wouldn't have to look at me the next day . . . or the day after that. Which he wouldn't have to do, because he was leaving.

Then a horrible thought hit me. Was he making his move now because he was leaving? Because no matter how things went, he would be safe?

Not liking the picture those thoughts drew, I tucked them away and tried to re-focus on the matter at hand. I'd almost died, for crying out loud! This had been my greatest regret, and I was trying to paint Ben as a bad guy so I could once again pull away? If I pulled away now, I would never know if Ben and I were meant to be. I had to give him a chance!

Yet one more worry tickled at me: we didn't have any protection. What if I got pregnant? My heart jumped and I realized I liked the thought. Ben would be such a great father, and I could travel with him and the band. It would be fun!

Sorry, God! I said silently, making my decision to finish what Ben and I had begun. *I know I promised you I would get baptized, and I will, but if I don't do this now, I will regret it for the rest of my life. Please understand.*

The moment I thought those words, a wave of ice coursed through me. As good as my body felt, my soul felt absolutely sick. A picture of Elder Wright once again came to my mind, and I remembered how good I had felt around him and

Gonzales. Their words had filled me with fire and peace, none of which I felt in Ben's arms—well, except maybe the fire, but this time it was a little different.

I don't know if what I heard next was an actual foreign voice in my head or just a very independent thought, but it said, *Today you choose the rest of your life.* This voice was followed by an audible one.

"I love you so much, Rhea," Ben said. "I can't tell you what it means to be the first."

The first. His words echoed in my mind, registering the fact that the way he said it implied he believed there would be a second.

Today you choose the rest of your life. If I could have shot the invisible messenger that delivered those ominous words, I would have. But it didn't matter. In that moment my heart broke, and the choice was made.

God, I take it back! I take it back! Help me do this!

"Ben," I whispered putting my hands between us.

"Don't worry, Rhea—"

"I can't do this, Ben."

He froze. "What?"

"I can't make love to you."

He made a strained noise in his throat. "Rhea, how can you not want this?"

An excellent question. One I did not have the answer to, so we ended up staring at each other while he awaited a response.

"Rhea, if this is about that promise to your mom, I think you've lived up to your end of the bargain. Don't deny us this now."

Any man will sleep with you. Save yourself for the man who will stay with you, my mom's voice whispered in my head. *I had three roommates who got pregnant, and only one of the fathers stayed around.*

"And what if I get pregnant, Ben? What then?"

That surprised him. "You're not on birth control?"

"No, Ben. Why should I be?" Even as he looked at me, I could see the desire diminishing from his eyes. He wasn't ready for a child. "Ben, let me up."

"But Rhea—"

"A promise is a promise, Ben." Only somehow, it had become more than that.

Ben hesitated only a moment before rolling to the side. I tried not to look at him as we reclaimed our clothing. Cursing, he tugged on his shirt, and I could feel the frustration pulsing from him when his hand paused on the doorknob.

"Tonight could have been great for us, Rhea."

I nodded my head. "A really big part of me wishes it could have been."

His brilliant blue eyes burned into me. "Then why are you making it turn out this way?"

I played with my shirt in my hands and tried to think of how to answer him. The only explanation was the truth, and I tried to express it in a way he would understand.

"Because I have to live with myself tomorrow."

His reply was to curse and storm out of my room, slamming the door behind him. When the front door slammed as well, the reality of the situation hit me, and instead of feeling peace, as I had anticipated, I was furious. Snatching the business card from my Book of Mormon, I dug around until I found where my cell phone had fallen in the madness and dialed the elders' number with a fury.

So a little voice had told me while I was on the verge of death that the Mormon church was true, and I had promised that little voice I would get baptized. That still didn't make any of this easy for me! Inside, part of me was still fighting to stay the me I had always been and screaming that I was a deluded idiot for heeding invisible voices and choosing emotion over reason. Because, let's face it, there is nothing logical about changing your life because of a feeling you got after two guys on the street—strangers—explained their religion.

Elder Wright answered on the third ring.

"Elder Wright?" I said curtly.

"Yes?"

"This is Rhea. Remember me?"

"Yes." He sounded like he wanted to be happy that I called, but my hostile tone made him cautious.

"Well, young man, what you taught me the other day better be one hundred percent true, otherwise you are in a hell of a lot of trouble!"

"It's true, Rhea. Are you okay? Can we come over?"

I said they could, gave him my address, and hung up.

EPILOGUE

I COULD TELL you the details of my conversion, but the truth of the matter is that it was rather quick and painless. Besides, when you promise God at gunpoint that you'll do something, you do it. It helped having the elders teach me things I already believed, and it helped me feel as if my mother were constantly by my side. I couldn't deny what I felt around the other Mormons I met, but I was rather shocked that people with such a proper image would have anything to do with me. After all, I wasn't exactly their poster girl for a "Choose the Right" campaign.

In that same three-week period I learned all the required lessons from the missionaries, Paul Bradley's trial date was set for October, and Keith's was scheduled for the beginning of December. Stephan Martel was no longer under investigation for embezzlement from his company, and a week before my baptism, I heard that Candace had gotten a promotion from administrative assistant to fiancée. I guess Martel found out that when the rest of the world doubted him, there was one person who never failed him and decided to make her permanent in his life.

Somewhere in the middle of this fiasco, I got baptized. It was a beautiful day in May when I entered a baptismal font dressed

all in white. Elder Gonzales met me in the middle while Elder
Wright waited for his turn to confirm me. Elder Wright had
been transferred from the mission home to a different city the
Monday before, but the mission president responded well to the
death threats I confronted him with and allowed him to come
back for one day only. Everyone tried to convince me to have
"ward members" baptize and confirm me instead of my elders,
but I couldn't think of anything more ridiculous. I didn't know
any of the men in the ward from Adam, and where had they
been the day Elders Wright and Gonzales cornered me across
from Paul's house?

Besides, if anyone besides Elder Wright—a hot guy who
didn't objectify me once and constantly begged me to "pray
about it"—had tried to teach me the gospel, I don't think I
would have listened. I guess I'll have to wait till I die to find out
if we made a deal in the premortal life. I think we did, because
when he laid his hands upon my head, I was filled with the
strongest feeling of recognition.

My father, my aunt, my uncle, Kay, and Emily watched
on, no doubt thinking that I had gone insane (to this day Kay
maintains that I joined the Church under duress), but they sup-
ported me anyway, and I love them for that. Camille laughed
at me when I told her I was getting baptized and then brought
me anti-Mormon literature the next day. I promptly handed it
back. The way I saw it, nothing good had ever come from her
in the past.

I tried to call Ben to let him know what was going on with
me but never spoke to anything besides his voice mail. I waited
for him to call back. He never did. Instead of pretending that it
didn't hurt, I prayed for him . . . and I tried to mean it. I asked
God to also let me know why He had not wanted things to
work out with us and to please help me heal. It would be nearly
six months before I discovered why Ben was avoiding me.

I quickly learned that refreshments are part of any Mormon

gathering, and after the baptism, we were led to the Relief Society room for food. Clearly uncomfortable, Emily bid me farewell halfway down the hall, giving me a half-hearted congratulations and saying she would see me at home. After eyeing the brownies suspiciously and seeing that I was otherwise occupied, Kay said her good-byes as well.

"You never cease to amaze me," she said as she gave me a hug.

"Yeah, I'm a little surprised myself," I replied.

"You aren't going to go Waco on me, are you? You start hand-sewing your own clothes and growing out your body hair, and I'll throw you in a different kind of ward entirely, got that?"

I laughed, even though she was dead serious. "You're the one who always said I acted like a Mormon, Kay."

"I know, but I never expected you to become one!"

"Who knows, maybe you'll be one too someday."

She laughed, but it was hollow, and her eyes grew dark. "Don't hold your breath. But one good thing is if I ever need a scoop on Mormons, all I need to do is give you a call for the fact or fiction."

"You can call me for anything. You know that."

"Yeah." And suddenly she was blinking back tears. "You're a great friend, Rhea."

I hugged her, since it fit the mood. "I wouldn't even be here if it wasn't for you."

"Yeah? Well, you saved me first. The way I count things, we're not even close to even."

I gave her a last squeeze and stepped back. "Well, stop counting then."

Her head shook, first at me, then with more concern when she looked around the room. "I swore I'd never come into a Mormon church. I can't believe you actually did this!"

I shrugged, knowing there was nothing I could say.

"Go mingle with your new clan," she said, shooing me away. "I'm being selfish. I'll see you later, okay?" But Kay didn't move. She stayed where she was, looking torn. "Seriously, if I'd have spoken up ten seconds earlier at that warehouse, you wouldn't have had time to make that promise to God to do all this."

That fact was going to haunt her until she died. Poor thing. "Yep," I said easily.

Baffled, she sent me an absent wave as she walked away.

I turned to face the room. Kay was right; the room was full of mostly new acquaintances who were all eager to speak with me, and all the attention was dizzying. Keep in mind that I'm a girl who spends the majority of her days in the shadows.

In the midst of it all, I did get two presents from my elders. The first was from Elder Wright and was a brand new set of scriptures with my name imprinted in gold on the cover. It was later that I learned that the book was far from free and had no doubt been obtained through a large sacrifice on his part. I accepted it gratefully and gave him a firm handshake in return. I couldn't wait until he was released in three months so I could give him a proper hug.

Elder Gonzales's gift came in the form of a secret. He pointed to the paperback copy of the Book of Mormon they had given me when we first met.

"Do you know the story behind the book?" he asked in his heavily-accented English.

Surprised, I shook my head.

"Well, Elder Wright is a very good missionary. You know this, right?"

"Of course," I agreed quickly.

"His whole mission, he hasn't had any baptisms. He works harder than anyone else I've served with, but no one has ever listened to him." I couldn't believe what I was hearing but didn't interrupt. "A few months ago, he got very discouraged and on one very bad day, he wrote home to tell his parents he was wasting his time and his family's money by being out here."

Shocked, I looked at Elder Wright talking to the bishop, seeing him through new eyes.

"His family wrote back about having faith and how the Lord was watching over him. Then later, he received a package. In it were very many things, including that book and a letter from his sister. She said she would fast and pray that he could find somebody. She said she would fast every week and pray every day that this book would help him find someone who would accept the gospel. She said that if he would listen to Spirit, it would tell him who to give it to."

My mouth was dry at this point, and I could only stare.

"He carried it with him everywhere!" Elder Gonzales said this as if he had somehow found it exasperating at the time. "I told him to put it in his pocket because it was getting ugly and the letters were coming off, but he always wanted to have it in hand to remind him of why he was here. For months he carried it, and that day we ran into you was very bad day. When he gave the book to you, I thought he was giving up on his sister's promise. After we left, I chastised him and told him he was stupid just to give the book to a pretty girl. Now it was gone! But he only smiled and said it was in God's hands now."

Needless to say, I was stunned. I was also crying, and the respect I had for Elder Wright officially broke the scale of measurability in that moment. I was also filled with gratitude for his sister and for God, who followed up on her prayers. That young girl would probably never understand how her actions had affected my life.

Suddenly I needed desperately to see my favorite elder. Excusing myself from Elder Gonzales, I weaved through the crowd of bodies until we were face to face. Then I did the biggest no-no in the book: I pulled him into a bear hug before he could protest. He was stiff in my arms as a few gasps sounded around us, but he did not push me away.

"Thank you," I whispered. "Thank you for being such an amazing missionary!" Only then did I feel his arms squeeze me back.

"Thank you for listening," he replied and, feeling the nervous eyes on us, I pulled away.

Clasping my hands behind my back so I wouldn't do something stupid like touch him again, I stood awkwardly in front of him. "I'm sorry, but I just had to hug you."

"I understand," he replied with a sympathetic smile, and we stared at each other for a moment, not knowing how to express the feelings that filled us.

"Thank you so much for everything," I repeated. Words were so weak. How do you thank someone for changing your life? What words can express the gratitude of another person stepping into your life and giving it meaning? For reaching into the rut you live in and leading you to higher ground? There aren't words, and I think that's why neither of us wanted to speak.

"I only thank God that I was the one who got to introduce you to His gospel," Elder Wright said modestly. "All that has happened in the past few weeks is between you and Him. I had nothing to do with it."

"You know that's not true," I said and cut him off with a wave of my hand before he could argue. "It was your legs He used to walk into my life and your voice He used to teach me. That was your gift to both Him and me, and I'm indebted to you for it."

He blushed and didn't have a response. Seeing how flustered he was, I decided to lighten the mood.

"Now get out of here and get knocking on those doors. You only have a few weeks left before you're back to girls and books and bills."

"Tell me about it," he said with a chuckle. "My girlfriend wants to get married the week after I get home."

"Really?" I said in surprise. I knew he had a girlfriend, but I hadn't even thought to ask him how serious it was between them. They were so young, after all. "How do you feel about that?" I tried to keep the concern out of my voice and wasn't sure if I succeeded. Twenty-one and married? I could only imagine how my life would be had I jumped into marriage that young.

He sighed as if frustrated he even had to think about it. "I think I'll wait a bit longer than a week. I'm excited to see her, but I'm different than I was before. I want different qualities in a woman than I did before my mission."

"And does she have those qualities?" I ventured.

His hesitation became his response, and he realized that I had caught on to that. "Don't get me wrong, she's a great girl! She's nice, she's faithful, and she is beautiful, but after teaching the gospel for two years, I want someone I can talk to on my level." I nodded, totally understanding where he was coming from. I couldn't imagine myself with a guy I had to explain things to. In fact, the combination of qualities I needed in a man were so complicated that they probably didn't even exist! "Am I insane?" he breathed. "Or do you get what I'm talking about?"

I nodded my head and said the words for him. "I get it. Sometimes we outgrow people."

He smiled sadly and shook his head. "Sometimes."

"I'm sorry," I said. Heaviness filled the air, and I decided it was inappropriate for the occasion, so I slapped his arm and teased, "But then again, you don't need to worry about that for a while yet, do you? Right now all you've got to worry about is keeping the Spirit with you twenty-four-seven and preaching from dawn till dusk. Am I right?"

"That you are, Rhea." His eyes appraised me. "You're amazing, you know that? You are too good to be true. When I write home in letters about you, people think I'm making you up. That is how much of a miracle you are."

What do you say to a compliment like that?

"Well, hey! I try," I said laughing, and in that same moment saw my father's eyes pleading at me from across the room. Two members had him cornered and were saying who-knows-what to him. He was fresh meat, after all.

"Have you met my father, Elder Wright?"

He glanced over to where he was cornered. "Not more than to exchange greetings."

"Well, then I think it's time I introduced you. I think he'll like you."

And together we crossed the room toward my father.

SHERALYN PRATT graduated from the University of Utah with a BA in communication. A gypsy at heart, she enjoys traveling and acquiring new skills. These days she can nearly always be found out and about with her dog, who has spent hundreds of hours watching her type. Visit Sheralyn online at www.sheralynpratt.com.